BOHEMIAN ANTHEM

SHORT STORIES
BY

ZUZANNAH L'ARK

 www.trafford.com

North America & international
toll-free: 1 888 232 4444 (USA & Canada)
phone: 250 383 6864 ♦ fax: 250 383 6804

Contents

"Je m'en allais, les poigns dans mes poches crevées;…"
Arthur Rimbaud

$\underline{1}$

THE BLUEBERRY PIZZA

What is wrong with me? She was asking herself after weeks of failing to find work, any work.

One of the last resorts was her idea to just walk around the neighborhood and see if anyone was hiring. There were some pubs and dusty galleries and an old fashioned one-person-behind-the-counter grocery store, a recording studio with a small stage, a fancy gardening shop, and a little farther by the Peninsula Park with a rose garden, there was a café. She went there to check it out.

It was empty, but a tall man with a thin pony tail was wiping off the counter, and wasn't opposed to ask his wife if she'd like some help in the morning.

"We are closed on weekends." *Ah, bon!*

When her family, her temporary host on Albina Street, left out of town for the weekend, she quietly cooked for herself a meal every time she was feeling hungry, using whatever she'd find in the pantry and in the refrigerator.

Nothing grew in the garden yet. Early spring nights felt still pretty chilly in this mild, humid climate which she wasn't accustomed to.

While she was designing her meal from the chosen ingredients, she was listening to a mélange of short, not very well reported news on the radio. The content was noticeably upsetting, listing local, pretty awful crimes, car accidents, cases of child neglect and such, and in the back of her head rose some questions – did she arrive to a good place? Where else could she live and work? Okay, here lives a part of her family, but she just couldn't make herself home in that town.

She's been here before; in fact, the first of her visits years ago left her with a pleasant experience, hopefully lasting for one of her daughters, who was thinking of settling down here. Visiting is however always shallower.

She felt in this town too far from everywhere. Perhaps, the proximity of the Ocean makes you feel like a grain of sand? Her hair, too yielded to the Giant; its salty, humid presence of 2.5 hrs drive turned her loosely wavy hair into curly, as if it was attempting to make of her a different person.

What if one should pay attention to how a place works from a much deeper point of view than work opportunities – there must be a set of qualities, by which one can tell this IS the right place?

"Follow your bliss!" was Joseph Campbell's reminder. She believed that also. Some people are lucky and don't have to go anywhere, she thought.

She turned on the oven and quickly prepared a shell for a quiche. As she was grating cheese into a bowl, mixing in cracked eggs, heavy cream, some cooked broccoli, and spices, looking for extra additional interesting ingredients, she discovered some frozen blueberries in the freezer. Hmm, why not to make a blueberry pie, too! And her memory brought out the last time she'd baked one:

It was for the Forth of July celebration, quite a few years ago with the neighbors and their kids in the village on the other side of the Country. The kids loved it, calling it 'a blueberry pizza'. She believed it was the last time she felt almost home anywhere, growing attached to the countryside with the river and lakes, orchards, horse farms, its pace, the closeness of several universities and their cultural influence, the presence of the independent movie theater, the weather of four seasons, and the fact she could have a cat. Nevertheless, it was getting lonely there. But the Bliss?! The 'Lusthaus', as would one philosopher call it also?

She pricked the bottom of the quiche with a fork in a decorative pattern, grinning for herself: no one will see this nice work; you'll cover it with the filling, why do you bother? And she answered to herself – well, just because!

She liked the playful approach, her capacity for delight was her strength, even under stressful circumstances, as if it was at the same time her refuge from the madness, in which the world seemed to have fallen during the latest years.

Or was she getting older and fed up with the jungle, where – if you don't adopt its 'sophistication', or at least wear a good mimicry – you were going to be eaten alive? She couldn't ever imagine she wouldn't work when she reached the retirement age as most people do. She liked working. What she didn't enjoy was drudgery; boring, uncreative, endless, thoughtless labor which sometimes out of necessity she needed to accept to make living. Sometimes? Lately too often, and now – none!

She poured the filling into the shell which fit well in the

rounded pie form, pressed the fork teeth in the pie shell around the edge for more decoration, and slid the whole thing into the preheated oven.

She admired her childhood girlfriend who was raising her three sons as a single mother, and was forced to move out of the city to her grandmother's rent-free country house with only cold running water and one electrical plug, where she cooked on a wood stove, where the winters were quite snowy and cruel; the little boys had to walk every day for about an hour in the dark, rain or shine, by themselves to the kindergarten, while their mother dragged on her back a huge bundle of tiny trees that needed to be planted that day. Every day, for many months. When they drove together some twenty five years later by a tall and deep forest, the girlfriend pointed to it:

"This is my forest; I planted it with my very hands."

She admired another person she knew ever since those early years, who wouldn't shy away to work manually, or drive a truck to be able to do his music, where he could express his whole huge, caring heart, even if he 'had to wait for 15 years' to release his first solo record. Follow your bliss!

She admired and respected tremendously her stepfather. He was a historiographer who deliberately left his position, because he'd refused the invitation to collaborate with the oppressive regime, and accepted employment as a manual worker testing water instead, often under very harsh conditions, and not making much money. She respected him for his heroic patience and silent courage with which he carried on, supporting at the times even her family.

The schedule of this hard labor allowed him at least to use a window of several hours when he could sit down, bundle up, plug in a little electrical heater in the freezing trailer, and write on his typewriter, working on his history assignments, published only as '*samizdat*'. He wrote out of love for his wife and her daughters (herself including) a little history book on their fascinating ancestry. Everywhere the job placed him, he'd search in the local archives for all relevant records on the relatives he could collect.

Soon, the officials discovered how 'easy' it was for him to continue doing his real work, and assigned another 'regular' water tester, who'd keep an eye on her stepfather, who then needed to always pack away his typewriter, and could bring only certain work in his backpack with him, that also contained the meals her mom had prepared for his week's absence from home.

And of course, she was reminiscing more while her quiche was beginning to golden, he was no longer able to invite any guests to break his solitary confinement, or review any of the drafts the dissent was quietly composing to make the fearful population aware of the moral disintegration that was taking place, mainly the human rights abuse not concentrated solely on the remaining intellectual elite, and to inspire ways of cultivating dignity, and to encourage and inform about practical and legal defense.

When she shared with him the detailed insights about her children's school, the fears to express any independent thought, the corruption of some teachers, when he saw the textbooks, namely the history textbook with altered and missing facts, and some out right lies, he simply said:

"Write about it!"

He was the one, who gave her the very first impetus to become a writer by simply saying – write. She understood – for the sake of the truth, for the record – write! Of persecution, he once remarked that it turns out to be always personal.

These people were a source of inspiration, strength, and connection for her. Gravely tested by life, like herself, there was never any need for a small talk. Even when they wouldn't face each other for years, when they finally did, only the external signs of aging spoke of the past distance.

She was most grateful for the luck in life to have been close to some of the most extraordinary, exceptional, loving and caring, honest, courageous – very few – people of her, and some of her parents' generations. When her stepfather passed away, she would daily miss him as one of her best, lifelong friends.

The radio was getting on her nerves with the reports of detailed horrific conditions for political prisoners in China. As if it knew what she was pondering about – the world has gone mad, or rather most of its people, but there is so much to love and appreciate, don't give me this distorted picture! And she lowered the volume.

The quiche began to smell very tasty, oh, she was getting hungry. As she was throwing together a tiny fresh vegetable dish, she caught herself singing. What was the song? Oh, one of the later love songs by her minute ago remembered close person! She tried to recall the lyrics, when the radio broadcast pulled her ears close again: an interview with someone who 'was in love with a poor rock musician, and was his lifelong muse and inspiration' and went on and on about the cliché 'sex-drugs-rock and roll'.

Bon Dieux, has the radio gone mad, too? Or has it turned into a parrot, mocking her thoughts? She couldn't hear the rest because two fire engines dashed through the narrow street with their sirens on. She covered her ears until the disturbing noise tapered off.

She reached and scanned the dial for another station –

none was any better, so she turned the radio off. The atmosphere in the house without a virtual human voice might lift the oppressive air.

Feeling hot and sweaty, she made herself a fresh squeezed lemonade, and opened the freezer for ice cubes. To her delight, she found some old ice with blue flowers in it, and she was happy to think her family had adopted her recipe using *borago* – or borage – for decoration. They must have totally forgotten about the borage ice buried in the freezer. Oh, of course – there was a long rainy winter.

She picked out the lemon seeds, and set them on a moist napkin; perhaps they'll sprout and she'll plant them, and it'll be a symbolic rooting ceremony for her as well. Lemon tree blossoms scent is one of the most pleasant fragrances in the entire world! Her lemon trees never had the honor of her caring presence to grow old enough to actually bloom, unfortunately.

She savored her lemonade and pondered in quiet: it's been nice to reconcile with her old gray cat owned by her family now. Her frequent moving in the late years prevented her from such an emotional luxury.

The cat enjoyed seeing her former and first lady as well, keeping a close eye on her feet movements. Aged and heavy, the cat was no longer capable of jumping on a couch, her lady accommodated to her needs, and stretched out on the floor near by. There…

Cats don't drive; they get splashed by mud as well as us, walkers, in the rainy weather, if water-amicable… Cats think in the four-foot mode, and distinguish between the people's two-foot mode and theirs, observing and predicting the near future by following people's feet's direction, often with their eyes almost shut.

Her cat used to prompt her by voice, or by her paw, when she would behave too cheeky, vexing the cat with neediness for petting her gray, striped coat, dotted on the belly. She was going to violate the cat's unwritten law of 'don't-you-even-think-about-coming-closer!' and sit or lie within the touch, imagining her stay in this house wouldn't be for long.

She and her cat used to be much attached. They admired one another as well. When bathing, her young cat used to visit the bathroom, and wished to try the bath as well, testing the waters with her paw and realizing oh, too much! She licked the surface at least, sometimes licking dry her lady's wet shoulder that was emerging from the bubbles.

The kitty was a foundling in blackberry bushes, blind and full of flees, abandoned by her family, which was cuddled together within the sight – if one had it – but certainly within one's ear and nose. That's why it cried so loud, day and night, sounding almost like an injured bird among the thorny shoots, where it was extricated from and brought home, fitting into her palm, she was reminiscing, and knelt next to the cat, sipping her delicious lemonade.

The cat's eye acknowledged her presence, and didn't object the hand on its back, giving a loud consent by purring. There were many intimate moments we've had together, was running through her lady's head, in the absence of someone she was missing: the bluebird-parents teaching their fledgling to fly, and her cat being very interested in watching closely the lesson, and almost getting the pudgy birdie for its toy.

A huge flock of all kinds of birds came screaming at the cat, that just couldn't leave the scene until the birds' cries called her lady out. The birds watched from a huge maple tree how she coached the birdie away from the cat, and how the cat got locked inside. In about fifteen minutes, the bluebird-parents circled a few times in front of her eyes to thank her for saving their child. It would be Paradise if we responded to one another like this most of the time... Praise the cats, she cheered with her lemonade.

It was time to pull out the quiche from the oven. She left the heat on for the blueberry pizza. It was to be a kitchen bonanza the next couple of days...

A sudden knocking on the door announced a man with a petition, collecting signatures. What for? Well, there is a new neighbor, a schizophrenic, and everyone's afraid she might shoot someone with a gun. Isn't she in the care of a doctor? The patient didn't want her old one, so she will need a new doctor!

She refused to sign such a dubious paper, and closed the door. So disturbing, a petition – for what, actually? To force someone to move out? Based on assumption? Or a slander...? Or, if for real in case of illness – is this place going backwards, still attaching a stigma to mental health problems? Or was it a nasty joke...? She was the only new neighbor, as far as she knew, in weeks... and she wasn't going to stay here for long.

Her heart was beating fast. In such an irritable state it would be hard to convince any employer of her competence to handle a complex set of tasks, proving it with one of her résumés, listing her rich work experience. Let's get the blueberry pizza together, baking has been always a calming remedy.

While the soft dough was resting and slowly rising in a bowl under a cloth, and the blueberries thawing to the room temperature, she prepared a mixture of flower, sugar, and butter which alone used to be her stepfather's favorite garnish on a pie – as she recalled. She could almost hear his voice saying: "People don't change."

What he meant was over time, in their essence. And as she was growing older, she agreed with his wisdom. Who was a good person in youth, she usually found good as old, too. And whose character showed subtle, but substantial flaws at a young age, at older age those traits only pronounced more – if the person wouldn't turn plain unbearable, or all together evil.

She was lucky. She still liked people, trusting that all were born with the same chance to be good – regardless of her frustrating experiences. She contributed that mostly to the lack of awareness. She addressed herself: has *she* changed, besides growing older?

Through the kitchen door, she could see the cat had shifted along with the traveling sun spot on the wooden floor in the big room next to the carpet, and hedonistically rolled onto her back, exposing her spotted tummy to the warmth.

"Would you mind if I joined you?"

Without waiting for the cat's answer, she lied down on the carpet close by, and shut her eyes. She realized how tired she felt, emotionally exhausted. How many times has she 'begun anew'? And yet – she always liked to think of one place she could return to, and call it home.

She couldn't help sensing it wasn't exclusive to her; it was almost like an underlined, unsettled, nervous energy she could detect in most people lately. It also seemed, everyone she spoke to admitted they were in doctor's hands, medicated. An overmedicated nation…

So, if the drinking water – as she just heard on the radio – contained flushed down, unused prescription drugs, she might get some with her lemonade, whether she wanted or not. But – each time the cocktail must vary, never the same!

Her quick relief to reinstate calmness came through her breathing concentration. With the exercise, there often emerged images, and sometimes fell a light, short catnap. The images stayed in her memory, quite vivid, and frequently turned out to be prophetic. Her body began feeling in one piece after a few long, inhaled breaths.

A distant female voice was calling somewhere. She thought at first the voice was calling a child's name, but after an inquiry with her folks, it turned out to be a cat's name. It sounded eerie, just like the first time she heard it:

"Eeee– moooh! Eeeemoooh!"

Could it be – See more! See more!?

She got up to check on her blueberry pizza dough. Through the window, in the midst of the vegetable garden with a few last year's stems and dead bad weeds, there stood a well dressed young woman looking like a model, and held a camera. She was really taking pictures – of what? Of that nothing!? Perhaps of that mole's hole? The female voice was still calling out – See more! See more! She refused to come up with an explanation and turned back to her baking.

The quiche looked lovely, carefully transferred onto a nice plate. She wished to have a company to share her meal with. The pie dough covered nicely the baking sheet, and the amount of the blueberries was sufficient. Hm, little too juicy, but the mixture of butter, sugar, and flour will drink some of the juice, she was thinking. And off you go in the oven!

"If it'll come out well, I could take a few pieces to the café as a sample, maybe they could use me as a baker!" she was pondering.

She thought of another inspiring friend of hers, she never met but corresponded with, who was in her mother's age, and became her occasional mentor, who – at the times of extreme poverty, having learned to be very resourceful in India – used to make living by baking pies, and bringing them early every morning to the market. Her fruit pies was a hit because she had built a clay oven in the woods, and picked fresh wild berries at a crack of dawn while her dough was resting. Another wonderful person in her life – how fortunate!

The friend wrote her a few significant, life changing letters, reminding her of a spiritual path.

"The next step might not be known to you yet", said one of the letters. With a great deal of visionary gift, in plain words, she wrote about the path in this life involving some major work. The recollection was resonating deep down with the seemingly obscured meaning, and she remembered *feeling* the light from before. It was coming in and out of the heart.

Oddly enough, she was reminded of her friend's predictions by baking her blueberry pizza. And thus, while baking it, she was reconciling the trivial and mundane with the hopeful sparks of the Divine. The tasty quiche could certainly attract at least the old Greek god's noses.

The present didn't seem to point her toward the next step on her path. Things in life appeared rather confused.
'Follow your bliss!' seemed out of reach.

The sunshine traveled across the floor, and the cat followed the sun like a flower and didn't mind her lady crawling near again, perhaps sensing its own days in this world were counted, of which the animals know a lot more than us. They both closed their eyes and fell asleep, a much needed cat nap.

In her short dream, she saw the neighbor's red pick-up truck and herself delivering a folded piece of paper behind its windshield. She woke up with a jerk, rushing to rescue the blueberry pizza from the oven before the firemen would arrive, alarmed by the smoke rolling through the windows. Nothing more inconvenient.

But it turned out perfect. She sliced it mentally: two thirds of the whole thing for her hosts, three pieces as the sample to the café, and what's left, she'll eat during her solitude.

Her night rest got interrupted several times. Disoriented, she got up; one time she needed a full glass of milk, and another time she turned the table light on, used her lipstick to create a print of her mouth on a piece paper, which she folded, and actually stepped out, placing it under the closest car windshield.

Finally, she was able to fall asleep, and nothing woke her up, until her cat's hungry mewing in the morning did. The tasty blueberry pizza for her breakfast, tuna fish for the cat.

From the near by church loud sounds of amplified service and the congregation's singing were heard. Several late coming folks, dressed in festive clothes and Sunday hats rushed in.

She was thinking about the past night, and how she kept waking up in the middle of it already for years and sometimes almost forced, or urged to do something quite trivial. She recalled now the milk during the night, and the lipstick imprint, and went quickly to see if the paper was still where she had put it. There were no cars in front of the house, only around the church. Hm. She wondered what the driver thought, had he found the folded paper. Then she remembered her brief afternoon dream with that content. How strange!

Maybe there was something underneath all this; she used to be able to understand the night dreaming. But she hasn't dreamt for a long time – except the last afternoon, next to the cat.

Her dreams used to be vivid, helpful, and many turned out prophetic, or simultaneous in connectivity with a close person. Maybe it was her soul trying to access her conscious mind, telling her something important, giving advice!

The night awakenings bore within a feeling of displacement, but her frequent moving might have been a good reason for this spatial confusion. Just like when a compass gets magnetized, and its arm doesn't point correctly to the North. Perhaps an afternoon walk would align her thoughts, and a *eureka!* comes on its own terms. She didn't mind the gray sky, and searched for an umbrella, just in case.

Her family enjoyed listening to the regular radio show for 'the people who like to eat'. Why not to listen today? There can't be anything much disturbing about recipes… The first time she heard it was in the car on the way from the airport, when she arrived. It was mostly about eggs, and one caller spent a long portion of his conversation with the host about hard boiled eggs, and how many different modes there were to make sure the eggs were truly hard boiled. She found that a bit absurd in the context of her life situation, but she liked to take advantage of any opportunity to learn.

"If you can't stand the heat – get out of the kitchen!"

Well, that's exactly what she did, didn't she: gone out to refresh herself by the lush, green gardens in the neighborhood. What a weird radio show today – she reflected, clutching the umbrella under her arm – about pet food, dog food! Meat, chicken, turkey, legs, wings and that's what some pet owners believed was all about love. The stories the listeners called in were concerned with fat cats, how to make them lose weight.

She thought of her family's old cat, who had grown so big, and suddenly a cold chill overcame her. The radio show – it was dawning on her with a delay, like a jet lag – seemed intentionally composed. And the name of the town where the broadcast came from to entertain a live audience mocked her name, as if she was supposed to be that place herself, all like a badly written attempt for a strange riddle with a humorous twist. What for?

She walked further to explore the neighborhood in the need of fresh air. The streets were named confusingly after various states. By crossing the freeway, using the high overpass, she discovered nearby an old firehouse with a huge tree in front, and a large parking lot in the back.

The firehouse was converted into a performing arts center and a gallery. Incidentally, there was a scheduled unveiling in a short while. She entered, and turned to the stairs.

One flight up, a long-haired woman wearing an old fashioned dress was attaching nametags to her paintings at the last minute. Their brief conversation about the show opening led its first visitor to the next room where an exhibit of textiles, arranged in a particular way, resembled a home interior.

She returned to the paintings. One by one, all in the 'douanier' style, but not very inventive, and rather made in a haste, were somehow stringed together by a strange logic. The line, as they were hanging, seemed to tell a story with irony and sarcasm.

Gradually, the underlined references began to cause her pain. One painting was titled 'Chalupa,' a painted attempt of a native boat, or a barque with a tent on it. To her, it suggested a home, that which she was missing. Another one pictured a wedding in the middle of a river, also on a boat. Food and gamble were other themes. Was that intentional?

Suddenly, two musicians rushed in, unpacked their guitars, and began playing Spanish tunes. She followed them to see what connection there might be between the flamenco and the rest of the exhibit, but the out-of-place looking musicians, perhaps Spaniards, or Romani men sat in a completely empty room, perfectly concentrated, and played to themselves with no one in there, and with no relation to the art. She seemed to be the only listener, but they paid no attention to her.

Was the whole thing another weird event during these couple of days, designed for her only to see? What for? To scare her, confuse, haunt her? Why was no one else there? The space felt lonely, stuffy, and self-indulgent. She couldn't take any self-indulgent art.

"Library briar bribery roses crosses *un croissant roi et saint,*" she was dispersing a nonsense with another nonsense, marching back, but with a nonsense of her own, which made a lot more sense, rhythmical, keeping the beat along with her steps. She kept on repeating the words around like a mantra. It cleared her mind of fear, worries, and anxiety, and aligned her with the quiet and regular pulse of her heart.

Nothing else happened. Just quiet and emptiness. A momentary void. What a blessing! Who doesn't understand this state, knows little about happiness.

And nothing happened during the night, no dreams, just a deep, long sleep. She woke up rested, relatively, reminding herself that today was Monday. *Provisorium* - restful?

The café patrons read the paper, or were doing homework, some of them chatted with the tall, still young but out of shape owner, who recognized and greeted the woman, who placed on the counter a neatly double-wrapped package, containing her blueberry pizza.

"Here it is – a sample: a home made blueberry cake or pie. Enjoy!" She needed to clear her throat, not having spoken much for a couple of days.

The owner took the package without a smile, and asked for her résumé if she had one.

"Oh yes, I almost forgot. It's got a list of various related jobs I've done. My profession is different, but I just need a job. That's why there are many time gaps in my résumé."

He looked it over; nodded and grinned at her, saying she was a traveler.

"We'll call you."

A small child entered, by the resemblance his, playfully wearing clear plastic cups on her bare feet. Glass slippers. She clunked toward a little bookshelf, and with difficulty pulled out a heavy book, dropped it on an armchair, and began to flip its pages. As far as the new potential baker could see, the book contained mostly photos.

She glanced around to see how the place's '*chi*' felt, and noticed upon leaving how eclectically it was decorated. A little bit of everything to please just about any taste. All natural teas, fair-trade chocolates, eco-friendly post cards, and black and white photos on the wall.

"How long have you had this place for?"

"We've moved in here a little over a year ago, but the business was founded about four years ago."

She walked out and strolled to the nearby park. Peninsula Park. No one was there, not a dog walker, not a baby sitter, not one homeless person asleep on a bench. All deserted.

Suddenly, a couple of vans arrived, and a bunch of shaved-headed men, and a few long-haired women spilled out and populated the flower garden. A man in charge distributed rakes, weed whackers, and other tools, and they all began working. There was something very conspicuous about their sudden appearance. Too organized, although one couldn't put a finger on it.

She pulled out a book, opened it, but couldn't read. In her purse, she also carried a small stuffed monkey, made so cutely that when it moved its head, the whole thing came to life – almost! She propped up the monkey on the bench. Why not? Look at people, we are not much more intelligent than you... *Homo hominem lupus*.

As she was thinking irreverent and ungrateful thoughts under the influence of uncertainty of any job, she noticed the odd behavior of the garden crew. In fact, they were no crew, but inmates guarded by unarmed civilians. They all seemed to try really hard not to look at her, but every once in a while someone did, and by some weird order, they all kept on moving closer to her, raking and digging weeds.

Suddenly and out of nowhere, another man joined them, somehow significantly climaxing the scene, but very shyly, aware of his exposure, and of an unpredictable task unknown to her. His hair was bleached blond, and she noticed his features. Her heart almost stopped in disbelief for a few seconds. This couldn't have been a coincidence. The man resembled too much of someone very important to her, now miles and miles away. In a few weeks his birthday was coming up, and she missed him.

What is this? Why is she witnessing this? Everything revolted in her, and she called out with all of her might:

"Heeeyyy!!!!!"

And when the bleached blond man looked up to her, more embarrassed, she threw him the stuffed monkey. He caught it, quite confused, and she was relieved by this interaction, knowing she was not imagining it.

"Throw it back to me, please!"

He did. No one laughed, but everyone stopped working, and watched the exchange; then the guards gave a quiet order to leave.

The leafless park turned deserted as before. As though something fell into water, and its surface closed and calmed down, and if no one saw this happen – it didn't happen.

Her retreat led her with sluggish steps, passing a trash can which the crew was filling with the garden debris. A mistimed, a little worn out red rose was placed carefully by the edge of the cylindrical trash can. Why? Who was supposed to find it?

"You've got a phone call from that café, mom!"
She lifted her eyes from editing her professional résumé with hope. The house felt really crowded, and with the baby on its way... If she finally gets a job, she'll move out to her own place soon.

"You can stop by any morning to talk to the wife."
"Even today?"
"Yes," said her daughter. She could see an unusual twinkle in her daughter's eyes. "I hope they liked your blueberry pizza."

The owner's wife was short, golden copper-haired, and called her blueberry pizza sample delicious with a European accent. A bonding touch, the baker thought with a relating emotion. She got hired; of course, part time.

During their brief interview, the little girl – without her glass slippers this time – brought over the same huge picture book and opened it, demanding attention.

The picture on the facing page was an enormous photo of a person with hands thrown to the sides against the dusty background. She couldn't determine more details, because the book was laid up side down.

"What is the man doing, ma? Dancing?"
Her mother shook her head, and apologetically smiled at her

new hire.

"No, darling, the man is running. Running away from what's behind him, you see?" said the mother calmly to the girl as if narrating a fairytale.

Now the new employee recognized what the book was about. All of the pictures with almost no text were taken in New York on September 11th of 2001. Why would such a book be there, accessible to a three years old child, why would the child pick it out of all the rest, more suitable ones?

At one quick glance, on that little bookshelf, there were mostly attractive children's books! Too weird, too weird. What's this street's name? Killingsworth…

The next few days her agile daughter searched for a suitable place on the craigslist; they called a couple of landlords, and set up an appointment with one – luckily in a walking distance from the café.

For some inexplicable reason, her daughter's language sounded quite irritated when she dealt with her. The mumbled, or even loudly pronounced lines like:

"Oh, you know everything! Don't you!" became quite a common place, as if her daughter was addressing someone else, and she, her mother, had turned into a different person during their conversation. She needed to move out as soon as possible, not to jeopardize any fragile, recently reconnected relations with her daughter, disrupted by her college years and travels.

The street address of the potential place was on another –worth. Ain't it weird? Weird again. If things weren't happening so often so bluntly weird, she wouldn't notice them.

The tiny apartment on the second floor had a minuscule, but nice kitchen. She could set up even a writing table there, find one or make one – going 'dumpster diving' like when her daughters were young. They all used to go around the neighborhood for someone's garbage that could become their treasure. The other day she found a small stuffed, but headless animal. She wouldn't notice it, but another thing happened at the 'free clothes' bin. A man on a bike passed by so strikingly resembling the same someone, just like the one in the park, to whom she had thrown the little monkey, that she felt propelled to call after him. The resemblance was more of a caricature, like a bad taste joke. Weird again...

She rescued the stuffed animal, and promised her little red monkey a friend after this tiny monster – or perhaps a knight who lost his head in a battle? – would quit being scary with a new head design, sewn on.

Childish? Oh, who cares! Life is more delightful that way. Low status? Laughable? Depends to whom. Who doesn't have a good, tasteful sense of humor, any imagination, any appreciation for the poetic perception, such person always remains a stranger to her.

She enjoyed creating stuff almost out of nothing. Her mom used to say – '*Une grisette!*' – a Parisian hat maker... out of almost nothing a charming head cover! *Et voilà!*

Her learning curve in the kitchen was rather slow. Her tall, young boss was no capable teacher. He kept taking frequent coffee&smoke breaks outside, staring across the street, as though the public library was the most interesting piece of architecture, or perhaps counting its visitors was his second job. His lifestyle reflected itself on his poor physical shape, and on his face below his shine-free eyes, underlined by dark blue circles. As if on strings pulled by someone else, he

24

was working quickly and impatiently; with the lack of his guidance, the work was quite frustrating for her.

She always considered kitchen as one of the more dangerous places, prone to injuries. The boss gave her often time consuming tasks, like huge pots to clean, but she was used to more terrible jobs from the totalitarian times 'at home', when she was kicked out from her profession, and had to wash stairs and floors in buildings for living to bring food on the table for her children and herself, having become – gladly – a single mother.

While she was now scraping the burnt soup from the bottom of a huge casserole, she thought of another girlfriend. Her proverbial taste in dressing up, in furnishing a house, her good heart, and hospitality were certainly missed.

Her friend considered herself a poetess, well read and smart. She could easily attend gatherings of writers during the dark era, when one needed to exercise caution about spending time in the company of people with dubious characters who were willing to collaborate with the suppressive regime in exchange for certain privileges. Her friend found it easy to communicate on a smooth note, and she used to joke about publishing an ad in the Personals: "Looking for a bad company to acclimatize."

Her admiration for poetry – in translation – went to poets like Sylvia Plath whose dark poems and her sad end of life the girlfriend regarded as inspiring. Back then it was more of longing for the world culture exposure than the fondness of depressing, however good art. Her girlfriend was quite a softly cushioned, beautiful girl from provinces with nothing disturbing in her life so far. A little voyeuristic admiration, a second hand suffering.

While cleaning those heavy pots, was she finding herself

in no position to write at the present time, wished perhaps for a little soft cushion, a little pampering, and that's why she caught herself at these jealous, mostly depressing recollections?

Was it the frustration of the drudgery after which she felt so exhausted, that she needed to rest, finding her head on strike? Were those the underlying worries about making barely just a plain living? Maybe. The solution might be getting a new notebook and a fresh pen, and schedule each day differently.

The spring was full abloom, she could be writing outside! Just like in New York where she turned the whole City into her hospitable apartment, bathing her feet in the Hudson River during hot days, or listening to the waterfall in the lobby of the Grand Central Hotel in winter while writing.

The Monday she came to work, both of the bosses sat quietly in the empty café, and worked on some papers. The side door to the cross street had a ply wood board leaning against it. She noticed a crack in the door frame.

"We got robbed overnight," said with an apologetic smile the little wife.

"Oh… Anything got stolen?"

"Just the change in the cash register, we don't keep any money in."

"Are you open?" the kitchen help asked.

The tall husband nodded, and waved his arm in a gesture: get you to the kitchen! Pots and pans lined up for washing were waiting for her there already. She was thinking what was the date today, and a jolt hit her – yesterday, when the burglary happened, was… The burglary happened on the birthday of the person she had been thinking of daily, but had no way to contact. Miles and miles away he was.

She peeked out to see if any patrons began to gather for their lunch, or students from the neighboring Community College came to pick up their orders during a break.

The main door from the street opened like on a cue, then two uniformed police officers entered, and marched straight toward her. Instinctively, she stepped backwards, her heart began beating fast. She had no explanation for this, and stood there as dumb as a puppet. The police officers froze for a few seconds, and as if on a remote control they changed the direction, turned around, and without one word marched off.

She looked at the bosses who didn't seem to have even noticed what had just happened, bent over their papers. Was that a coincidence, the burglary and that May date? Weird, weird again!

The rose garden smelled so nice with the colorful, gradually opening buds that she didn't mind the stressful reminder of the past visit, and entered to sit for a while on the bench under the large, space filling sycamore tree. She carried in her bag the red monkey and his stuffed friend whose new head resembled more of an innocent looking piggy, rather than the assumed former bear.

In her disposable camera, there remained about six pictures; she decided to create a picture series of the two new friends. Ridiculous maybe... By the fountain, in the blooming tree, on the bench... She was curious how would the arranged poses turn out. An idea for a children's book, perhaps.

As she was playing, she noticed more people coming to the park, populating the area at an even pace. She stopped what she was doing, and kept looking. Obviously, these people weren't there by chance. Her heart began beating faster from the discomfort.

The most striking seemed the dogs and their owners, and how they interacted, as if always maintaining their presence in her view. One man was throwing plastic discs to the dog in the fountain, and the dog was fetching them repeatedly with the same speed and rhythm, as though the whole scene was a cartoon, and not life.

A young woman, almost without any sound, passed by with her dog, perhaps a golden retriever; also rather floating rhythmically, like directed by a metronome. None of the people would even glance at her, as if she was invisible. Her discomfort grew, finally she simply picked up her bag, and walked away without one thought of trying to speak to any of the people. No one talked to anyone else either.

The following days at the café got slower, the patrons thinned out, no one could tell why. The owners looked exhausted nevertheless, and somewhat dreamy. Their house got under some kind of a disaster spell too.

They owned seven animals. One morning, with another of the apologetic smiles, the wife shared with her kitchen help that their cat ate their bird, their dog ran under a car, their snake escaped, their turtle disappeared, their rabbit ate something bad, and they didn't know if it will make it. The only unharmed was some kind of an exotic slow-motioned, not very cuddly pet, and the cat that got scolded for eating something else than its cat food.

Suddenly, the husband announced that they were going to take vacations, and they no longer needed any help. But they really liked her blueberry pizza. No one has ever asked her to bake it.

2

ORANGE COOKIE

He introduced himself by sneaking in through the crack of I.'s door. Amorously and with an expression of apology, he circled quickly her room glancing at I., as if saying – and now, finally, we are alone, what do you say?!! I. said only – Well... welcome then!

With his head lowered to the carpet, he inhaled all the news; after all, I. was a new tenant, a new neighbor. He better finds out about her all he can ASAP!

He was still very young; his Egyptian head was adorned with pointy ears, his slim, long, elastic body swiftly checked all the corners, gaps between the few pieces of left-behind furniture in I.'s studio, and measured all the chances of open doors to another space.

Then he elegantly positioned himself in the center of the room, and began systematically cleaning himself, as though he had dirtied himself during his tour.

I. was so taken by his conscious excitement about the visit which seemed premeditated, she withdrew herself from all she was trying to do. He sensed her watching him and acknowledged it; as an actor rewarding his attentive audience, he came closer, and allowed I. to pet him. Under her hand, his muscles felt athletic. He was giving in I.'s rubbing every which way.

I. never met a cat that wouldn't begin purring under her hand. But this one wouldn't. Perhaps he didn't know how to, perhaps he forgot, perhaps no one has ever rubbed his back, behind the ears, and between the front paws. He was in the state of awe. He decided to jump on I.'s bed, and ponder on this experience.

They both could hear from the first floor a woman yelling out through the open house door:

"Kitty, kitty, kitty!"

His alerted ears made him stand up but then, he abruptly relaxed and swirled himself into an orange ball on I.'s bed.

I. opened her walk-in closet door quietly, and searched for her snapshot camera which had a few pictures left. I. has been taking random pictures for months to record her thoughts, unable to write yet. Her surprise visitor certainly deserved to be recorded. When the camera lit its automated flash, the cat's ears warned the rest of the cat, making him open his right eye. Nothing else moved. He went back to sleep. The room got instantly swollen with peace.

There's something about the second floor and hanging between the earth and heaven that allows this omission of gravity, or worries perhaps, however temporary or imaginary. A good company allows us to do what we need most - even if it's just sleeping.

It felt wonderful to be someone's good company,

regardless of I.'s visitor honoring her with just a nap. Even though her visitor was merely a young cat, I. honored his need to sleep, thinking he chose to come in to find peace he might not have where he lived, the place called his home. They'd treat his visits as such, but won't turn I.'s home into his, I. decided, mainly so, because she didn't feel at home there herself.

From the garden, a loud yelling and screaming broke the quiet again. The cat only shifted his weight; the familiar quarreling couldn't disturb his rest when coming from an audible distance, perhaps only reminding him of his chaotic home where he would find his bowl with food. Hopefully.

The boys were screaming in the garden, as I. could see from the kitchen window, naked under the stream of cold water from a hose. These wild, often violent games prevented the other housemates from using the garden.

The kids never played one game for long, never quietly, but always carried some kind of a weapon – a stick, a plastic sword, or some blinking, rattling, monstrous, light-shooting machine guns that were often dropped and scattered on the stairs, day in day out.

Whenever I. encountered the playing boys in the hallway, they would often stop as though they clicked on the pausing button of a computer game, and without greeting her, with a blank stare as if I. were a ghost, they'd return to their mute shooting instantly, right behind her back.

Before the family with four kids living below had moved out, the six children played together – the two oldest youngsters babysitting the four young ones.

Quite often, I. passed through walking up and down the stairs and caught a glimpse of their games. Sometimes, the two boys were sitting on the steps in the hallway leaning against the railing, just like on a gallery in an opera house, and the two neighbors' little girls were lifting the curtains on the French doors, 'performing' naked for the boys who watched them fascinated and breathless.

One time I. went inside the next door apartment on her floor and saw how squished the two boys' family lived, then she understood why their mother decided to take the vacant apartment downstairs where they lived now; even more evidently, since a new baby was on its way with the mother's new boyfriend.

The mother always smiled in people's presence, and spoke loudly and cheerfully on the phone almost all the time. When she didn't think anyone was around, she'd scream at her boys, and reprimand them constantly. She wouldn't greet I. upon bumping into her, unless I. initiated a small talk. The mother looked at I. with suspicion; she couldn't help it, I.'s even so slight accent branded her as a suspect.

The neighbor ran soon out of the topics she could talk about with I. who showed her interest in kids, letting the neighbor know she worked as a temporary teacher. Perhaps the neighbor could relax around I., if a middle school hired her to teach children, there's nothing much weird about the stranger in the house.

More noise coming from below inside the house chased I. out for a walk. The boys were fighting now over who was going to bang their fists on the piano. No reprimand for that. The orange ball on I.'s bed lifted its head, reading answers in I.'s face about the noise.

"We better go outside, kit's..."

As I. was descending the stairs, she glanced through the uncovered French doors of the boys' new family room and released the bewildered cat out ahead of her. The scene there was clear: the open piano which no one ever really played was now abandoned, the music sheets propped up – all for a happy display. The boys have gone on some new fight, and their mother was smiling and chatting on her cell-phone taking a sun bath on the deck.

The cat took off dashing to the opposite direction, choosing the path toward a barking dog behind the tall plank fence. If I. knew his name, she'd call on him to diffuse his panic, but his name remained a question.

I.'s pain subsided so much she could do a few stretches on the grass in the Rose Garden Park. I.'s world has shrunk during the past months, after her body gave up on her and the vast world had moved inside.

I. would have never believed she could lie in bed for weeks motionlessly without being able to read, or even listen to music, let alone write, hardly sleeping, and survive this trauma without hating herself, or crushing her skull from pain against the wall. Instead, I. embraced the ever-present, overwhelming, inevitable pain, and accepted it as her close companion, and learned how to master it with an invented breathing technique with somewhat aviatic, self-suggested images, and still humbly love life.

The whole situation has amounted as an avalanche. I. has gotten even poorer than before when she had no income, with the temporary teaching position now barely paying for the necessities, but I. was proud enough to buy own food instead of going to the food bank where people loaded their cars with bags and sacks of mostly unhealthy groceries.

I. preferred counting her supply of 'nine beans/day' like Steinbeck. Except I. couldn't eat beans: indigestible for her stomach. Lentils served as a good substitute, unfortunately causing an aftermath in the audible world. I.'s French female friend from a long time ago used to announce the sound preemptively, assuring a laughing reaction instead of an embarrassment:

"*Attention! Je péte!*" So – *Pas du faux pas...*

People turn away from you when you are miserable, better keep the misery to yourself. Later, they will reproach you that you didn't ask for help, secretly relieved you didn't ask, indeed. And they quickly sweep their guilty feelings under the rug: thank goodness, she's well!

Later, they might fix their shameful embarrassment by surprise presents: you receive a gift basket shipped from far away. Only when you open it, oops, the fruit's rotten, for it had been packed in for long weeks, thank you very much; you can't help thinking: oh, a Christmas sale! You're then expected to send a thank you card, nevertheless, and avoid mentioning the condition you found the fruit in.

The grass under I.'s body looked lush, but felt sharp and rough; it smelled by chemicals. The roses just began opening their buds, the birds were chirping high in the sycamores, and the linden trees held their heart-shaped leaves above the outstretched, thin, fingerlike, ready to go flower-bearing stems with tiny bullets at the end.

Hopefully, the bees will show up, they say the bees are disappearing, and some clever heads think of the solution: transport of the bees to the areas absent of them. All the bees would go mad from the spatial confusion, wouldn't they? Very easily imaginable: I. almost did once herself.

A quiet rustle under a tea rose-tree drew I.'s attention. Oh, a gray rat was playfully exposing its body to the sun, completely oblivious to her presence!

I. jumped up and glanced quickly around if any small children were playing in the grass, but I. was the only one. Babies were probably asleep at this hour. I. regretted she didn't bring her snapshot camera along. The rat picture would be a nice company to one of the cat ones. The rat in the roses, the cat in the bed. Better than the other way around. Well, maybe not, who knows.

The gate by I.'s house was constantly broken. This time, a broomstick was holding the doors from the inside. I. had to give a holler, and it took several times before anyone came to open.

The pregnant mother smiled at I. sweetly with a simultaneous crease in the middle of her forehead. She was slowly duck-walking to the gate to release the broom stick. Her aloofness mixed with an obstinate suffering in her condition elicited I.'s thanks tinted with guilt that I. had bothered her with calling to be able to get through the gate which was almost collapsing, and she was the one who'd fixed it so cleverly with the broomstick. Again, I. thanked her.

She enjoyed conversations about problems. And she liked to tell I. about her solutions. But I. was wrong. The gate was held by the broomstick not only to keep it from falling, but from opening as well.

A golden puppy was running in the garden on the loose. It dashed toward I. from behind the house to greet her, and jumped up to I.'s face with its floppy tongue hanging to one side. It got yelled at angrily right away, but it didn't seem to mind at all, and just ran back again. Proudly, the mother said:

"It matches our carpet and the colors in the living room."

"You'll have full hands with the baby and the boys, and now the puppy..."

She embraced her belly with both arms, and sighed:

"It's getting heavy... that's because they are twins!"

"Congratulations! Does their father know that yet?"

"He does... But those aren't mine, didn't I tell you? I am surrogate. I am doing it for friends. I love being pregnant! I can't wait to be their second mother and participate in their lives!"

The first thing which flashed through I.'s mind was all this new furniture and equipment brought in the boxes a few days ago... Oh, this was a paid job!

The kids in the garden were galloping around wildly, until their mother yelled from the top of her lungs:

"Stop it! I am tired, I am pregnant, that's enough, Indigo! Navy, quit pulling the puppy's tail, NOW!"

The mother gave I. a charming smile, lifted one hand, gently raked through her blond hair, and then she seductively lowered her eyes and whispered:

"Oh, these boys!"

I. has never heard the boys' names before. I. has never noticed her lisping before either. Maybe she used it only for being charming.

The house seemed to be in pain, as though unable to tolerate any longer so much noise. The steps were creaking, the whole structure rickety, holding together only by many layers of paint. Perhaps the house took upon itself some of I.'s pain.

I.'s few potted flowers looked like wanting to leap out of the window. The tiny bathroom served as a refuge in times like these, as the quietest room in her place. The only dissonant element there was the loud fuchsia color paint.

When I. went first shopping to the closest food co-op, she realized the wild colors on the walls were identical with those in her place. Match! What a coincidence! A tenant from her apartment was hired to paint the store, and then they used the left over paint from the store at home, or the co-op hired the person who used to live in I.'s place to do the paint job, and they wanted to share selflessly their wild color taste. I.'s place though was so very minuscule that it was more probable it got painted with the leftover paint from the co-op.

The co-op people treated customers like old-time patrons, and it made I. coming back more than anything else: everyone who worked there was unique and accepted, disregarding the amount of tattoos, earrings, years, fingers, or hair. The food people could look as alternative as one might imagine, but in their hearts I. detected a slumbering, tiny, little bourgeois looking for good food, fun, comfort, security, and a retirement package. Is anything wrong with this kind of happiness?

Only one guy was an exception. He walked around this alternative world without piercings, tattoos, head-phones, earrings, with eyeglasses out of style, often sweeping the floor, or stocking the shelves with supply, solemn in this lively place, speaking with deep, quiet voice, gentle, shy, slim, and well read. It was always a pleasure to start a conversation on any topic. Soon, it became clear why his ash-color hair was blond, but looked tired, discolored.

I. was really curious why such a young person would be so somber, namely when his inner voice finally imprinted a lovely smile on his serious face, and for a brief instant he resembled a boy. Having aged in one lump sum at age thirteen when his father died, his shoulders ever since carried the burden of responsibility to look after his four younger siblings. Their mom couldn't take it from the time their father came back from Vietnam, and started to drink.

He was at the cash register when I. entered, escaping again from her noisy house. He greeted her with such warmth that I. began feeling some suspecting glances from the rest of so very alternative staff. She hasn't been there for months, unable to walk this far.

I. realized why she felt close to this gentle soul. He reminded her of someone whom she eternally missed; not by the visage that much, but by his loneliness, friendliness, lack of prejudice and ego, and because of his wisdom gained by the life experience. He hasn't traveled the world, but could picture most of anything to the detail.

He embraced I., a sparse commodity in her life in those days, and introduced her to his younger brother whose shiny soul just filled the space around. I. had to take a deep breath, and hold in her tears. Two brothers who silently loved each other. They stood there, chatting in low voices as old friends, and savored this loving energy in a triangle with equal distances. Not for long.

From behind, a muscular girl reminded of herself intimately to the younger brother, and almost brutally interrupted their conversation, as if making sure I. wouldn't maneuver him into a dark corner and hide behind the shelves, trying to unzip his pants.

The younger brother politely introduced her as a girlfriend skipping 'my'. After she left them alone again, the brothers told I. about a pilgrimage to India the younger brother got invited to undertake by his guru. Was that why he had avoided to call the girlfriend 'mine'? Did she know?

I.'s ash-blond friend mentioned that his little house was going to be deserted, because his brother would be away for long, worrisome months. How about the others in the family who might need a refuge in his house? But no, they all stood on their own feet firmly these days.

I.'s feet began to serve her better again; the sunshine broke through the clouds more often, and the air was so very pleasant, full of fragrances from the trees, bushes, flowers, so that one got almost hit by a blow of scent and had to search against the wind to find its source, whether the source happened to be an inconspicuous dark-leaved laurel brush, or acacia, linden, cherry, or other trees. One needed to turn the head up almost to the sky, or to the scents of flowers below the knees.

I. learned to walk tall, literary as well, because the strain on the spine, on its nerves, and the ligaments was alleviated that way, and her muscles liked to be used. It contributed to her sense of being reborn.

Often looking with new eyes at the same things required a double take in disbelief that they were still the same, because I. had such an ordeal behind, and has shifted inside, not only in space and time, but also invisibly so much that I. doubted sometimes own visibility.

Her perception of the invisible aspects of life sharpened, keen in both, very little and very large distances, in material as well as non-material. I. could sense various energies emitted by human intentions, feel the presence of life-giving, or life-supporting forces. Animals, kids, and old people efficient in their ways either from necessity, or due their finer attunement with the nature responded to I.'s presence with peace, and pleasant engagements.

With adults this was rare, and most of the time unexpected, because it was rather seldom when an adult lingered in engagement patiently, often subconsciously. Adults don't wish to know who they are most of the time, they react as if they got lost in a labyrinth, and disengage themselves quickly, frightened. Yet, there's no peace possible in the world without going in that labyrinth, and believe in Ariadne's thread, that is finding one's way out too.

I.'s way was the lessons she'd assigned herself for to earn a non-visible, unrecognizable master degree in being a loving human. Every fortnight, I. received a thick envelope with its content which she needed to study in quiet, do homework, and practice various exercises twice a day. That suited her lonesome existence well.

A peaceful energy like a thick field condensed around her when she practiced her quiet agenda, and it was difficult for any disturbing ripples sent her way to even tickle the mind with a negative thought to give birth to a negative emotion.

Working backwards into the past with the help of the sunny peace, I. no longer reflected on the past as something capable of casting a shadow over today. I. was learning to live today, making today the most important and most awake. I. needed to keep this thickness of peace with her at all times. In this world full of egotism, falsehood, greed, thirst for power, one could feel very vulnerable when walking around with own naked soul, on their inward journey.

Mindful of not throwing pearls to the swine, I.'s only task would be to distinguish between the like-minded and the swine. And as the life has taught her, the two were always in the close proximity. She realized the need of walking about the world disguised. Unadvertised, in fatigues. Invisible, or so visible that it makes one invisible. Like a fata morgana. Write under a pen-name, *le nom de plume*, or as the French say – '*un nom de la guerre*'; it was similar to a war.

Walking back from the food co-op those several blocks lined with gardens and trees, crossing the noisy, dusty streets where its corners accumulated indescribable filth, symptomatic of neglect, that kind of indifference always made simple questions arise, like why do people throw garbage on the ground? In the medieval times, there was no pavement, or very little left from the Roman Empire conquest, and the toilets were latrines, if at all. Doctors just began to understand the circulation of germs in a larger density of population. In Europe, plague and cholera were rampant. Defenseless, fearful people... in a stinky world.

And hundreds of years later, we still don't live up to the discoveries, the gifts the best minds left for us to inherit and utilize. The connection between the filth on the street and health is seldom made. And we still get easily possessed by fear, I. thought.

How nice it was to see the other day a mid-aged, bright-faced lady with a back pack bending down to pick up garbage on a trendy street in the fancy part of town, making a remark that before she'd get to her destination, the street would be clean! Here, in this part of town, hands of one pedestrian wouldn't make any difference. Diverting a river through probably would. Better to turn one's eyes upwards, to the sky.

When I. did, she noticed a pattern in which the clouds were lined: they looked like painted in a regular order. I. recalled her co-op, ash-color-haired friend's sermon about the artificial formation of fake clouds created by the military airfare he had researched on the internet which in his view was the new security paranoia, not for the purpose of hopeful rainmaking to solve the nature's drought threat.

I. forgot about her neighbors completely being vaguely reminded of their absence by the stillness and silence.

The phone alerted I. about a message by its red flashing

light. Wow! Someone actually called her and left a message? Rarely someone local called this number; I. was still a stranger in this town. Maybe, a reminder of the chiropractor's appointment, I. thought.

During her bed-bound months, I. was trying to imagine what it might be she could be doing when – and if – she recovered. The time spent on the internet by researching how folks with disabilities made living, wasn't very efficient. I. wasn't just hoping, I. was determined to recover fully, regardless the chiropractors' doubtful prognosis. What? Sick? For the rest of her life unable to dance? Never!

Yet, I. was struck by the fact that during the past several years, all of her minor injuries – like a cut eyebrow by her sunglasses when she fell down tripping over a poorly finished sidewalk curb, or a persistent shoulder ache caused by a clumsy dance partner, or a burnt forearm while ironing, or a scratched knee from another fall, or a twisted ankle during an exercise – they all happened on the right side of I.'s body. The excruciating pain got also hold of her right side, waist down.

The recorded voice on I.'s answering machine had a British accent, and asked her to come in for an interview. I. could design her class anyway she wanted. I. could even set her price. Appreciation in the European style? Or perhaps desperation? Did someone quit?

Behind her door, a quiet scratching announced a visitor. Oh, Mr. Cat! Come in!

I. was so relieved! I. was close to get work in her field! No more kitchen help, no more ZOO gift shop sales, no more ever so lovely nursery plant care with hummingbirds' regular visits, and also with an old fashioned boss.

Daily, he'd bring donuts at ten, and you better ate them because what he'd give you to do in the afternoon; you needed all the energy you could scrape out from your aging, and weight gaining body after so many motionless weeks in bed. The labor assigned to you would leave you absolutely exhausted till the next morning!

I. heard another sound from the floor below. A voice of despair, sadness, and fear: the baby dog left alone. Let's go see it, Mr. Cat.

The golden puppy was tied to the back of a porch railing confused by its sudden singleness. As soon as it noticed his visitors, it began barking wildly, hopefully, and happily in its puppy-expressive voice.

"They can't leave you home alone, you see, you might soil the matching carpet, understand? It wouldn't be matching anymore. Kitty, do you want to meet your doggie friend?"
But the orange tiger took off, darting to the opposite direction.

When I. got closer, she realized the dog tore everything within its reach to pieces. It wanted to play, chew, laugh, and obey someone in charge. Its ears got all wet; it drank water from his bowl, and the water was all gone, because the bowl got accidentally knocked over during the fight with an old sock, dropped on the way from the laundry room in the basement.

"Hi doggie, let me give you more water!"
His ecstatic, joyful reaction moved I. Her face got licked again, and she became an instant friend.

"I've got to go, but I'll come to see you again, okay?"

His penetrating, sad crying started as soon as I. disappeared from the puppy's sight. Why do people acquire pets that aren't intended for petting?

Surprisingly, the bus ride to I.'s interview didn't take too long, considering it crossed the bordering river to another state. Suddenly, a weird pattern in all this dawned on I., especially during the last few years. Something was working against her, some toxic influence depriving her of using her education, gifts, loves, and inclinations. Talents, enthusiasm seemed to turn into an unfinished business too often.

In this town, I. has conceived already so many good ideas, a few really good business ideas based on her desire to create more beauty and harmony. All too often I. found out a few months later, someone took over her starting business on a big scale, investing money, and basically wiped out her humble and naive – I. admitted that – beginning. How many more times? Well, this is America, free enterprise, ideas are a goldmine, so one shouldn't share any, mainly when they are excellent, right?

I. has always enjoyed inspiring teamwork, collaboration, sharing, so keeping secrets where it called for cooperation made never sense to her; the constant failure to build and develop a great concept, and invest her time and effort in something valuable to only find it stolen later, over and over, was painful and frustrating.

I. started teaching to make a living, thinking even if someone got 'inspired' by what she was doing and how she was doing it, those 'copy cats' shouldn't make her nervous. I. believed it was the personality of the teacher that made the course unique. The hope she finally came up with own thing almost impossible to duplicate filled her with a new energy.

The place looked dirty and neglected, I. thought, but it took upon itself the pretense of high society. The chandeliers only used every other light bulb, yet the dim light couldn't conceal how dusty the hanging cut glass pieces were.

The gloomy ambience was enhanced by the navy paint on all walls. In one instance, a spider suspended itself quickly from the ceiling, checking I. out. She wasn't sure if the owner of the agency saw it, and that was why she ushered her speedily to the room where I. would be holding her classes.

I. handed to the British lady her résumé. It was obvious right away she had no clue about the quality of I.'s experience, however British she sounded. When I. asked, the lady explained she had moved to this area from Australia. I see, was all I. said. It seemed more like a desperation than appreciation. As long as I. was going to be in charge of her agenda without interference, she was going to stick it out she decided, hoping to be fit enough to work.

There was music coming from somewhere, live music, blues or gospel, for certain. I.'s slow, ponderous steps tapping on the sidewalk began to blend well with the rhythmical accompaniment.

It wasn't dark yet, and the fact that I. happened to be in an unfamiliar part of town didn't discourage her. She got drawn by the music inside the building like by a magnet. It turned out to be a church not immediately recognizable from the street.

Everyone there was involved in a passionate singing, yet almost everyone noticed I.'s entrance. With the exception of one white couple, all folks were black, dressed up for the occasion, including festive hats sitting on the ladies' heads. One lady without interrupting her singing peeled herself off of a pew, and approached I. with her arms spread:

"Honey, welcome among us!"

She spoke with a distinct Southern accent, and finished her

welcome with a big, warm hug. Suddenly, tears leaped out of
I.'s eyes. She has been holding tears for so, so long, and this
was the place to cry and sing at the same time. I. knew the
next song to her surprise; it came almost like on a cue:

"Give me that old time religion..."

The musicians were quite young, and really enjoyed
playing gospel music for their community. A nicely sounding
harmonium, an upright base, percussions. I. guessed they
wore different jackets on other nights in a jazz club.

I. came as refreshment toward the end of the service,
and the musicians liked to showing off, improvising. A well
harmonized female trio sang their grand finale so powerfully,
that the church walls resonated. Everyone got up, even the
elders, and all of them holding hands finished the song
exclaiming:

"Thank you, Lord!"

It felt natural to I.; she recalled how much she always
wished to visit 'a black church' but never dared, because she
wasn't sure if the black congregation would let her stay there.
That night I. fulfilled her old wish by a slip of music, so to
speak. Hallelujah!

I. wiped off her tears, and received a big smile in return from
a little boy whom she didn't see before. He just rose from the
wooden pew where he was resting.

He was holding something in his hand. Their eyes kept
connected, and he decided to show I. what it was he was
holding. They were two little plastic soldiers, red and black.
He turned them secretly toward I., and began shooting,
laughing, saliva streaming through the gaps between his
missing teeth. His bright yellow T-shirt read in the red letters:
'Lord, Save Our Troupes!'

The pastor concluded the service with a prayer for the

safety of those who served the country. I. felt like an intruder into the congregation's privacy. Perhaps their own children got taken. I. said her prayer hoping to leave the church unnoticed, but before she did, a man took a quick picture of her with a snapshot camera. Flash!

I. left hastily, confused about the last event, and again feeling out of place, not belonging anywhere. She felt guilty for being white, a misfit to the little boy whose dad might have been fighting somewhere far away. I. was wondering what that snapshot meant. Did someone get nervous about a sudden stranger in their house of Lord?

Thus pondering I. noticed a creeping, unpleasant feeling which slowed down her walk. Before she could carefully open the wreaking fence at the house not to knock down the whole thing, I. had realized how much she wasn't looking forward to coming home.

Still quite tired, I. stretched onto the bed where she had spent many weeks motionlessly recovering. This wasn't home in the slightest! And will never be! It was a temporary shelter, overpriced, and confining, not cozy, no matter how she tried to cheer it up. *Une mansarde* – one could kid oneself thinking of Paris.

Why has it always been such a tremendous chore to make a living? Far from the intelligent concept of the path of the least resistance?

So – what are you going to do about it? Live in a tree for free? In an empty wine barrel – without morphing into a cynic, *pardonnez-moi*? The thought made I. chuckle. She turned her head over her shoulder to see if the itching on her back meant feathers, if she was finally growing invisible wings.

The few possessions I. owned have considerably thinned out during the last several years, while she was moving from one place to another in increasingly shorter intervals to create work, or find some, just to survive. It was quite amazing to realize how little one needed. Yet – it seemed that the soul was suffering from not relating enough to life, since there wasn't enough peace, safety, restful time.

Not out of sentimentality I. included in her bundle a handwritten letter in a blue envelope and a picture, both of which at some point got soaked in water from a burst pipe, being stored in someone's basement between her two moves. But I. wouldn't throw them away, a huge piece of her was attached to their message. Then there was a little old porcelain angel which traveled with her all over, wrapped in a clear bubble plastic for fear of breaking it accidentally; another piece of her preceding the soaked letter and picture, but related like lovers.

The angel's face was serious, her wings gilded, and she was standing on a fluffy cloud, found years ago in a dumpster during the whole town clean-up. I. always wondered how lucky she didn't get shattered in there. It's been so long ago, I. couldn't remember if she ever named the angel.

The only regret I. admitted weighing somewhat heavy were her notebooks of handwritten notes good for nothing, her own records of perceived observations, many of them, no longer easy to transport around the world. I. worried she wouldn't be able to retrieve them, and they might get lost, or fiddled with, if found, without her permission. Without own editing, necessary for reading the scribbled notes properly, they would give a very fuzzy account of her, and the events.

I. also missed her books. She was thinking about them with distress, since her time was used up laboring for survival, not for reading, such a luxury, and searching for paid work by all means available, mainly by a vain surfing of the internet.

I.'s only exposure to words – other than own disquieting thoughts, often composed of expressive particles like hmmm, uhuh, wow, shhhh, uhhhh, and such – was her listening to the radio. Quite old fashioned – and 'practical': one could at the same time cook, for example. I. would turn her boom-box almost automatically for the BBC news, sometimes for music. Listening to the music always asked for I.'s full attention – music refused to be just a background.

When she was so ill, the stereo was her only companion, the connection with the outside world. I. began to understand how the inability of experiencing first hand might distort the way of thinking. The war news bringing daily casualties, the dead count, compared to the inspirational, uplifting programs were disproportionate, spreading anxiety.

I. consciously stopped this line of thinking, having realized how many times a day she led such unfinished conversations with herself, and how for that reason they remained also quite smudged, unrefined. What happens to the brain?

Recently, she passed by a sports bar. Through the door ajar she saw everyone inside watching a loud game on a huge screen, the game was running as well on their laptops. Simultaneously, she caught a glimpse of some other cartoon-like game jumping on one screen, and on one table, by a tall café au-lait, spread papers and a textbook were suggesting the guy was working on a test for school which took another part of that laptop screen. I. was hoping he wasn't into a medical profession, or another involving lives of people. He might be mixing the football lingo into his assisted suicide paper.

I. could persuade herself to go to the library, and borrow a good book to read, or visit a second hand bookstore, one of her favorite activities – yeah, and get her there another volume of the complete Shakespeare's works which she ended up leaving behind several times for their weight; but I. was still struggling with a guilty feeling of investing her time into the indulgent, 'impractical' activity, such as reading.
Irresistible however, as well as letting Mr. Cat in whenever she would hear his pounding on her door.

I.'s walking after her painful illness was giving her pleasure, adding one more of the simple pleasures to her repertory of joys. The joy of movement, the appreciation of feeling the air with I.'s whole body, the awareness of senses of which her skin seemed the strongest, for something magical has happened in her healing.

I. has realized own strength, and appreciated it as a gift. She decided to learn more about it, and put it to use. This brought up a whole new way of thinking; not about survival and making a living, the most common concept of a lifestyle. Yes, money is needed; income should be coming IN, not be dumped all into bills, that's indecent. There must be another way, of course a legal way.

In the meantime – as absurd as it could be – I. counted the change in her pocket for the next bus ride, and squished her activities outside the house as efficiently as she could into two hours for which the transfer was valid, not knowing that just a few months later I. would turn into a plain pedestrian for many more months to come.

Teaching someone something engages one's faculties in such a way that one becomes own pupil, I. found after a while of designing her curriculum for the children in the agency. I.

expanded the classes for all ages, hoping to be able to offer her experience in different settings.

Finally, I. bravely invested her time into reading, suspecting that she was doing it *de facto* to quench her thirst, rather than out of necessity to prepare the lessons for which I. wasn't getting paid.

The children joyfully accepted I.'s coaching, a little too demanding for their weekend fun, but the classes left them interested and willing to come back with their finished homework. I. asked them for writing a brief skid, or thinking about certain more complex topics, sometimes initiated by making lists, like their ten favorite things.

Their answers reflected limited experiences. I. often found herself walking all the steps toward them, rather than meeting them on the way. I. was learning about the youngsters thoroughly, almost for the reasons of being able to foresee their advanced life.

One twelve years old girl wrote on her list of ten best things – similar to most of all of them:

"#1 mom, #2 dad, #3 my brother, #4 Monica, #5 Center Plaza Mall, #6 my cat…"

When I. asked about #5, she said:

"It's my best #5, because in the Center Plaza Mall, there is everything!"

Another girl passionately disagreed:

"No! It isn't! You can't buy any food there!"

But she beat her with:

"Oh, yeah, there are food quarters!"

And that was the end of it. One bright girl's hot list got corrected:

"#1 mom, #2 dad… No, wait! I forgot! #1 God, #2 mom…."

The kids began to discover themselves and I. enjoyed creating and teaching her dynamic and innovative classes.

All this wasn't going to last. I. got paid with checks that bounced a few times, and her bills remained unpaid, causing a domino effect which only worsened her previously difficult financial situation.

Something strange was happening. The agency wasn't prospering before I.'s involvement, and now it seemed going bankrupt. I. didn't understand it, and the Australian owner's shifty eyes suggested I. wouldn't hear any explanation from her either. It was time to look elsewhere with the well designed workshops.

I. hasn't seen Mr. Cat for a while, she thought. The puppy has grown in the few months and was allowed inside the house more often. The opportunity arrived one evening, after I. came from her last class at the agency. Her neighbor was getting in the car and I. asked about their cat.

"You mean Cookie?" she called through the rolled down car window. I. nodded, so that was the cat's name!

"We no longer have it. It got hurt badly by a car, and the vet's bill was going to be too much, so the cat was put to sleep." And she took off, probably rushing to see the twins to participate in their lives.

I. stood there with tears in her eyes not believing what she was hearing. Mr. Cat was in heavens. Cats' Paradise for orange Cookie. I. couldn't shake off an overwhelming, painful feeling of a sudden thought that had occurred to her: was it possible that whatever her heart held dear was prone to get hurt?

In I.'s head a list of ten most loved ones began to form, except Mr. Cat wasn't there, the list seemed to be in the chronological order – but no surprise, I.'s checklist contained mostly losses, heartbreaks, and hurts.

Standing at the gate propped up by the broomstick, I. talked herself out of the painful sadness by saying: you aren't alone in this!

I. heard a quiet barking from somewhere. The golden puppy was tied to the wooden railing by the laundry basement entrance. I. went to cheer herself by saying hello to the lonely doggie. Both of them missed Mr. Cat who perhaps never felt home in that noisy house. Just like I.

The next day became the day of searching for everything: work, place, and hope. I. called the food co-op if they didn't need anybody part-time. Fill out an application! Goodness, starting all over again. No time for what wouldn't even pay the bills!

What was on her list of ten best things? What was *her* #1? If the kids came up with their list, I. must be able to do that as well, no? All she found out by attempting to make the list of ten best things was that she feared to wish for the best! Why?! It seemed her best was related to so much loss and pain she refused to even think about it! Children don't develop such a self-censorship, until they are no longer children. Why did it all seem like walking in circles?

Below on the deck, in a bright pink bikini bathing suit, the voice of I.'s neighbor led a long cell-phone conversation with someone. Her piercing tone of voice broke through I.'s thoughts with particles of her stories explaining her life to someone in a strikingly pragmatic manner.

Her boyfriend moved out, she would have a babysitting business during the rest of her summer using the garden… Isn't that great? Free enterprise. Loving kids!

In the meantime, her boys began to wreck the house from the inside without her intervention. The puppy joined them with wild barking, and I.'s neighbor – without changing her position – yelled out as loud as she could:

"Navy! Indigo! Cut it out! Puppy, puppy, stop it!"

The dog was nameless. Perhaps its owner ran out of the shades of blue? The orange cat's name was Cookie, regardless his color. Don't children like to give names to things and their pets?

I.'s family used to name their kittens by the alphabet: 'A' Arkasha, 'B' Betynka, 'C' Cecil, all the way to 'P' Pimon. Osvaldino was graduating from high school with her. She was wondering if the twins got blue names as well – Azure, Aquamarine?

Life seemed to be happening at some other place. A quieter place. Much quieter. It was time to find it.

Listen to the heart beat…

3

MOVING AGAIN

"This is Freedom!?" announced a voice.

"Pardon me?"

"Freedom Child."

"Oh, is that your name?"

"Yes. So, how old are you? If you want to be considered for living here, you need to be well over forty."

"I am in my fifties."

"Oh, good, just like myself."

"So... there's one more person living in the house?"

"Yes." The voice on the phone paused, and acquired a veil of mystery. "My roommate Paul... He is in his late forties."

"Well, I'm glad we've finally connected after playing a phone tag for a couple of weeks."

"Hm. And... Which part of Europe do you come from...? You said you had family here?... And what do you do?... Self-employed?... I guess you can tell me when you come over."

It took quite a few blocks to walk from the bus stop to the address. The avenues and streets were mostly on the grid. The National Land Ordinance required a long time ago to build cities in the Roman way, West from the Ohio River; contrary to the streets on a hillside along which the houses get built, where the roads are curvy and snaky, like the paths made by thirsty cows walking to the river, according to the law of the least resistance. The muddy trails got eventually paved, like in Boston.

But we weren't on the East Coast. We were far, far West, walking on Portsmouth, Riverside, Lombard, and St. John's streets. What kind of revelation will happen today?

The streets didn't always cross or connect. In this part of town, it was tricky, you needed a map. If no one told you, you might never find your destination. They all seemed the same – small houses, painted with bright colors, over time faded, sunscorched front yards with a few evergreens cut into grotesque shapes, a villainous fashion of the past years.

Lonely, hungry cats crossing the streets here and there in a slow motion, as if never met their enemies – cars, perhaps because the gasoline prices got so high… due the war, which felt very distant here; almost no one drove these days.

What jobs could these folks hold? Shipping-receiving, light industrial, shipyards, heavy burden lifting. After a day's work, who wanted to go to an uplifting show or a concert?

On the main street, those few bars and pool joints got packed at night, and the police patrol were the only vehicles on the road, ready to interfere with the numbing nightlife.

The Chinese dry cleaners on the corner meant a lonely representation of an above average expense for one's business attire, a luxury expense these days. Curtains and shutters covered the windows at night, and through the gaps and cracks, blue reflections of a hundred some television channels would seep in the sidewalks. 'Videorama' might get some business. Movies. Cartoons. This is a country with a cartoon mindset. Violence presented with a smooth, floating motion. Harmless, you can laugh! Live shows on stage exploited cartoons and animation for an animated audience, doing the right thing, instead of animosity. Who goes to see live shows these days…? This pink house must be It, matching the picture on the internet.

The door opened, and a wax color face filled the crack, expressing expectations mixed with curiosity. The face crystallized into a fixed dead-end emotion. Deep lines aside her nose and mouth changed the shape from downward to a loose 's', and two rows of big, somewhat neglected teeth let out a breathful 'Hi!' between them.

The daylight illuminated her shirt with a cold pattern in blue, green and yellow from the seventies, washed out but ironed. The only signs of any motion in the still neighborhood, were her dark, beady eyes in the stiff face, and they were piercing the visitor's face as if extracting all her life into a capsule for later use.

The dark doorway yielded to the wax-colored face with a forehead hiding under large, oversized banks. A thin, short ponytail brushed her collar in the back. Then finally a bony hand holding a piece of paper enlarged the doorway.

"Hi – Freedom..."

"You said.... Was your name Joann?"

She began waving a piece of paper, accusatively pointing out the discrepancy, and sat down to a table. A quiet, old sewing machine matched her shirt in color.

The visitor stood still, not invited to sit down. It allowed for noticing every single movement in the house, even behind its walls. Nothing was breathing. Nothing was moving until a sudden, slow, almost lazy movement in the middle of the table made shift the visitor's eyes quickly.

A large bowl with a bizarre face of convexly enlarged gold fish was bulging in the clouded water. It seemed to be greeting the visitor. It couldn't be overlooked; as if the fish was screaming for help.

"Well, I just don't use my name in the emails. Friends know that," tried to make peace the visitor.

The gold fish's eyes were fixed at the visitor, as if shooting a home video, or taking pictures of the rare occurrence – a guest in the house. It kept on complaining, but its owner spoke over as fast as possible, trying perhaps to obscure what the fish was bringing up.

"It's not the matter of explaining or correcting," said the owner of the gold fish. *Her* name was Freedom Child. "It's a matter of disharmony. I don't think we would get along."

The unmoved visitor didn't want to leave without seeing the house after spending an hour to get there, hoping to learn more about the mystery of being a house mate of absolute strangers.

"Well, could I see the room?"

"You sure may."

Freedom led the visitor to one of the doors, and without using a key to unlock it, she just turned the knob. The small room was surprisingly full of furniture. Freedom sat up on the queen-sized bed, and her hand was smoothing over the cover which didn't need to be smoothed over with an undisguised tenderness.

"Yes, she said she'd come with a truck to move her stuff, but she hasn't. She's moving in a condo with her boyfriend."

Her hand was lovingly reaching behind, as if someone slept there.

"On the picture, there were no bars on the window."

"Just because you didn't see them, it doesn't mean there were no bars."

"All I saw were the lace curtains."

The tiny room was dark; there was no 'plenty of afternoon sun.'

"I don't remember how the picture on the internet looks like." She surely didn't seem to want to rent the room!

Off to the dungeon! Steps to the basement... It took a while to adjust to the sheer blackness.

"Here, my roommate Paul lives," she pulled together the edges of the curtains behind which it was so dark that even if Paul, or anybody slept, or sat there at the moment, one couldn't tell. Freedom initiated the next point in the tour.

"Here's the smaller shower we like to use," announced she, turning the light on. It smelled by the lack of air. A couple of big, hairy spiders got panicky when Freedom came close. Did they only hide away for the time when the two took a shower … together? And then the spiders rushed back in the corners to restore their torn cobwebs?

Freedom's face was obscured by the darkness, but her voice revealed pride and suggestive emotion of satisfaction, because she'd already made up her mind. This was her house, and the visitor was no match. Now was her time to show all of her treasures, because they would remain hers, only hers. There wouldn't be any interference from another woman, exotic woman, whose breasts were as interesting as her eyes, her voice misleading as her final handshake to which Freedom hurried by ending up her audience back at the table.

Satisfied with herself, she could get back to her sewing machine, mending a man's shirt, something to do while waiting for a reply to her job applications which she'd been putting out there for months.

"The values in this world are all diseased!" She gave her final lecture, pointing to a chair. "Would you like to sit down? Can I get you anything?"

"I'll accept the chair, thank you. No, I'm fine."

The gold fish opened its mouth in the glass globe. A sudden darkness of enormous size breathed into the room. A black hole. A way out. A way in. Deep silence. A loud shriek for life.

"If the world was brought into one human body, it would be cancerous, ill, hopeless, monstrously warped, and shapeless. I don't like what is happening, everything is just for profit, it's sickening."

"Why to walk around complaining? Looking at the world's sickness with a magnifying glass, and get the view out of proportion?" quietly stated the visitor. Freedom's beady eyes caught on fire:

"I'm glad I don't have children! What a world to live in!" said Ms. Child, free from children.

"I think it's good to have children, there's hope, no?"

"All these punk-rockers!!!"

Maybe the fish was singing a punk rock number:

"Free lo-ove..."

Maybe the fish was yawning.

"I don't mind them."

"You don't?!!!"

"No. I have kids of my own, and they are great."

Freedom Child, the gold fish, and even the sewing machine froze with their mouths open. Each of them thinking something. The sewing machine was counting the minutes before Freedom Child would sit down to her project of finishing the matching, protective covers on the chairs, sofa, and a couple of pillow cases for Paul's bed; that would keep her employed. The gold fish called for fresh air, fresh water, fresh life, and an ear to tell its story to. And Freedom Child herself was thinking aloud about the new tenant, being rather a man. "A hetero man." (Hm.) Why not to move Paul upstairs and use the big shower?

The visitor got up feeling foolish about spending so much time on something so unworkable which her intuition had suggested right at beginning. She could have corrected the impression made with her statement about the punk rockers saying she was also a grandma of one, but she chose to let it go, because she agreed upon one thing with Freedom quietly:

"It wasn't about being correct, it was about disharmony."

"Thank you for unlocking the door for me," said the visitor looking forward to the breeze outside. Freedom outstretched her arm and teeth, still sitting down:

"Oh, you're welcome."

They shook hands. For the first time, at last.

"How warm and soft your hand is!" exclaimed Freedom.

"Hm, maybe that's who I am."

The gold fish closed its mouth; perhaps that was the end of the story.

As the door was being shut behind the visitor's back, the recollection of Freedom's hand unwilling to shake upon welcoming the visitor flashed back through her mind. Yeah, she only offered the back of her hand – hard, bony and cold.

"Confused," pondered the visitor.

Confused about the present, not having dealt with the past, as though we all have bought the lies which are choking us, and we are hungry for the truth, screaming for fresh air, water, life, and a listening ear, unable to leave the cumbersome boxes, full of dust behind, and begin anew, light, so we can fly again.

Why not admit to it – we are all... homeless? Scared, without feeling love? We construct own, heavily guarded, little universes to build an illusion of home.

4

THE EMPTY NEST

European, single, mid-aged, all that Karla needed was a room in a peaceful house. It took lots of time to find such a situation. Now she was living in an old, spacious house, on its third floor.

The house had a good *chi,* regardless of overflowing shelves, crammed cabinets, nooks, corners, even whole rooms filled with antiques which 'we, Europeans' would call rather rubbish and nick-knacks of dubious value.

The good *chi* was a result of the fresh flowers the landlady would stick daily in vases, cups, jars, little cute dishes, practically into anything capable of holding water, and she'd place those all over the house, even in the restrooms.

"Yeah, one restroom is downstairs, right around the corner. Count there all the frogs you find!" called the landlady's husband with his thunder-laughter after the new tenant.

"Oh, she loves her frogs!"

The new tenant has never seen the landlady leaving the flowers behind, maybe some green fairies were in charge of the tiny, fresh, fragrant, and colorful miracles when no one was watching. Maybe she, the landlady, was counteracting the stuffiness of all the objects that represented some dead relative, however dearly missed.

The new tenant's European eyes always landed with surprise at a new tiny flower spot near her chair in the dining room so quietly cheerful, matching the flower or color pattern on the table or around, as though the strength of the female spirit and inspiration created a poetic way of survival under the harshest circumstances, even around something like:

"Do you know Costco, dear? We can take you there, whenever you need."

These were the landlady's husband's ideas of educating the Eastern European immigrant about the Land of Plenty. He'd speak in a loud voice, assuming she would understand *his* English better.

"Thank you, I don't like Costco," would Karla reply firmly.

"Then we won't take you there," he'd say with a hidden sarcasm, turning it on his way to the kitchen into a patronizing chuckle.

"I like eating organic."

"So do we," tried the landlord to win the competition over his European tenant. "My wife is an excellent cook. But when you try to raise three children," and he would slide a huge empty dish with some bright red, trembling remnants in the kitchen sink, and continue with his explanation:

"I love *my* diet Jell-O."

Then he'd go back to the massive leather sofa, lie down, and cover himself with an extra large, heavy, quilted blanket, glancing at the new housemate while she was eating her simple dinner. He'd sniff and inhale the smell passing by Karla from the top of his 6 and 1/2 feet, hoping she'd give in his repeated suggestions about the benefits of sharing food.

Karla was trying to demonstrate her autonomy by setting her plate with love and respect for the gifts of life, and prove her healthy diet good looking, too, juxtaposed his lifestyle.

Watching television from his vast sofa, the television with its screen taking up the whole wall of their family room, the landlord would flip through the channels, stop at one with volcanoes vomiting flames, and stare still, fascinated, with his mouth ajar. His puffy face with kid's cheeks glistened, reflecting the lava eruptions. He sighed, mumbling as he was falling asleep:

"I love *my* volcanoes."

Filling the void was what the landlord was doing with his television screen covering the living room wall, and his wife with many flower dishes and vases, and both still shopping in Costco, transporting the boxes of groceries up and down the house many months after their three children had moved out!

The landlady was busy all the time. At night she'd sit down with a book, in the morning she would devout her quiet breakfast time to reading a paper almost daily, the New York Times. Then, off she went.

One runs life as a parent in a mechanical way, occurred to Karla, on a schedule, and when the children grow up emptiness might creep in.

Karla was asked to stand in. Maybe they weren't aware of it, since the landlord wheeled and dealt and bargained, he nevertheless treated this void with a non-negotiable force, because he was scared finding himself powerless, like a commander who lost his army.

"What is the life supposed to be about now?" they might be

asking. How do we look to the outside world? Assumed from the landlord's brief speeches he advertised the neighbors with to her – writers, professors, travelers, doctors, real estate brokers – 'all very successful': Karla never met any of them. The many mentioned house parties hosted around this decent neighborhood, Karla was usually told about after the fact. The couple never went to any of them, but the landlord would brief her on 'the fun'. Why, it remained a mystery.

The landlord's good wife began to decorate the house for the upcoming holidays: pulling out boxes from the attic with their festive china, carrying the boxes up and down the stairs multiple times, catching breath with her husband cheering to her efforts from his leather sofa.

"Have you found any room for those, darling?"

And then waving his paw at their new tenant, who would enter after a few unsuccessful attempts to unlock the house door:

"How's outside, dear? You got blown in by the wind, huh, hahahah?"

His laughter almost blew Karla back outside, hadn't she slammed the door behind herself quickly.

Some of the Christmas garlands were already sitting on the spare chairs, like patients in a dentist's waiting room. Karla mumbled something in response, and under her breath told herself while she took in the fact:

"Hmmm, Christmas coming up! It'll be really something new in the total strangers' house!"

The house was built more vertically than horizontally, as if the original settlers began with digging a hole in the ground to survive their first winter, and the next summer they laid a foundation on top of that 'zemlianka', and never enlarged the base.

The next floor then also only offered just so much room divided into tiny spaces, and the next year – when the family grew bigger – another floor was added onto the top floor, and finally another one, as though no one looked at the house from the outside, but always felt their way upwards somewhat internally, or dreamt about the addition lying in bed.

It reminded Karla of one English story about children who lived in a tall house, and wished to grow up quicker. Somehow they got hold of a medicine which made them grow so fast that their necks pushed through the chimneys, and that was how they could talk to one another: with their heads sticking up above the roof.

When Karla finally climbed all the stairs and lied down on the sky blue carpet, she could see the naked maple tree with just a few remaining red wine colored leaves, courageously hanging on and flapping in the strong wind.

The tree was her visual refuge, helping her to remain a part of the natural world with birds and squirrels visiting it, and building their nests on it. The tree crown, even with so few leaves covered the whole window's view. It made Karla feel just like one of the birds, lying on the floor, like flying with her wings spread. Often she'd play a game with herself, imagining which bird she was today: a song bird, a nesting one, or migrating, of field, backyard, forest, beach, but she never thought of birds of prey.

The wall color was pink. Karla didn't like it at first. It was as if one slept in a candy box, she thought. But then the slanting sun rays inflamed the maple tree, and the reflection of the burgundy and golden leaves gave the space such an illumination of unique color shades of warm light, that she would catch herself rushing there, trying to return on time as much as possible daily to experience the atmosphere.

As if the light was bringing in some news that couldn't be delivered in any other way by some photons of undisturbed quality, reinstalling so much needed peace and tranquility.

The sounds of the house were muffled by all the floor levels, and so her time alone was very quiet and private which she was almost ecstatic about, feeling grateful to the builders, she pictured as those kids with their necks sticking out of the chimneys to be able to talk with each other.

Before would Karla descend the stairs to the kitchen, she always almost subconsciously peeked out of her window if she'd see any of the cars parked up in the drive way to avoid the small talk with her landlord. Her impression was that he got assigned to her by some unseen authority to reform her, re-educate her, and prepare her for some kind of a role she already knew she'd refuse to play.

Hearing him in his all-owning mode, listing all of *his* property, unavoidably seeing him daily snug under *his* quilt on *his* massive leather sofa, falling asleep in front of *his* television screen covering the whole wall of *his* living room into which one happened to enter straight from the street, and finding *her* food disappearing from *his* fridge, *her* conclusion was that *his* philosophy about women was mainly concerned with how to use what they had that *he* didn't have. Yet!

If nothing else, at least their resources, and even better if they spent a part of it on food, and cooked it in *his* kitchen, shared it, and stored it in *his* refrigerator, then – if they happened not to be *his* wife – then *his* wife could take care of *his* very important affairs, and could have more time attending for example to the administrative part of *his* software business (usually carrying boxes of *his* stuff), recently down-sized to himself, one partner, and an office (the shelves in *his* basement, next to *his* washer and *his* dryer).

The basement was the first hole in the ground dug up by the original settlers, Karla thought.

"When you do your laundry, dear, notice how many computers and software parts are down there! It's *my* business; I am an expert in a not-too-common brand, I could rebuild your computer! And make sure you let me know when you do your first laundry, because you will need a little tutorial on *my* washer and *my* dryer; it's a science, and they both are a state of art. Not that a housewife wouldn't be able to learn how to operate them," he'd chuckle, entertained by *his* own joke.

I bet your wife must have gone through a few of those lessons, thought Karla.

"*My* wife loves *my* washer and *my* dryer! She wanted exactly those, so she got them. I paid cash for *my* washer and *my* dryer," he clapped with his huge palms each time, sounding like a small thunder.

The landlord has learned to speed up his speeches. At every occasion he spoke faster and louder, but each time also longer as Karla passed by, because their bumping into each other became less frequent by the new tenant's design.

Karla gradually abandoned any specks of politeness, or any pretense of patient listening, demonstrating her freedom to move away from his authoritarian, reforming attempts. He simply believed that because things were *his,* he was right about everything, especially in *his* territory.

His wife managed to lure him once a week for a short walk around the reservoir and into the woods on the hill, but he would not leave *his* cell-phone at home. He was very attached to it. At home, he would wear a small pouch which he'd never take off, resembling a shooter with his holster.

He'd stuff his loud phone conversations with a kind of

technical gibberish full of incomprehensible words which he was very proud of.

"I love *my* cell-phone, I wish I didn't have to carry it. I always search for it when it rings, and if I put it into the message mode, it feels really funny, it's ticklish. I haven't found yet the best spot, so if it were a part of me... but then no one would see how cool this one is!" he claimed with a childish pride, lowering his eyes, almost blushing.

"Then you'd be a robot, no?" was Karla's slip of a tongue.

"Hahahah!!!! Did you hear it, sweetie-pie?"

His voice now followed his smiling wife, carrying heavy boxes with food from Costco.

"Yes, I did, Dew," uttered his wife catching her breath, but still smiling. "I wish you had a 'GO' button installed for me to push when it's the time to go for our walk!"

Hmmm, why people take themselves for a dog that's a mystery to me, thought Karla. Oh, Dew!? Did she hear accurately? Is that a nickname, or revenge of his mother, possibly father, or a full parental conspiracy? Wouldn't it sound almost lewd if one was that kind of an imaginer? Could it be she called her husband 'dude', and Karla didn't hear her addressing him correctly?

During the next few days, the Christmas preparations suggested the landlords would have guests, in fact lots of guests over: all three children back from college for their recess, some family friends, and traveling acquaintances.

"Oh," tried the landlord to stop Karla on her way upstairs one afternoon. The light was especially bright, because the sheer clouds came with the wind from a rare direction, and she was looking forward to her lighting show in her room.

"Oh, I would like you to spend Christmas with us at our

dinner table, so you feel like you are a part of our family," shocked the landlord Karla with his authoritarian kindness. It was not even a question.

"There are going to be perhaps about ten of us, the dining table can seat up to eighteen. My wife is not only an excellent cook, but a host and decorator par excellence. Oh, by the way, a few more people will sleep in the rooms on your floor and share the bathroom with you – just for a couple of weeks, and then we all fly to Hawaii."

"Thank you for your generosity," said Karla, and began immediately counting in her head where she could spend Christmas, losing again her feeling of being home anywhere with such an imposed pressure on her privacy. The landlord assumed a solution for a single person's way of celebrating holidays.

"I might need to cat-sit," said Karla with not a very persuasive tone of voice. She turned promptly toward the stairway, and climbed to the room upstairs before the sun would decline too low, before the maple tree would darken in the cast shade, and the special effects of the light reflections no longer pleased her heart.

Upstairs, Karla dropped everything by the door, and lied down on the thick carpet, spread her arms and felt it, appreciating the clean feeling. In many of her previous living spaces the quality and cleanliness of the floor posed quite a problem.

She loved to exercise and rest on the floor. Sometimes she needed to make her bed on the floor out of necessity. It really bothered her to find tiny irritating bites on her neck below her hairline in the morning! When was Karla looking for a new place, she found always better to have no carpet in her potential place, than a dubious floor covering.

The tree was still absorbing the defused sunshine, the wall reflected the slanted salmon light, and the room offered an atmosphere of repose. Suddenly, she understood this wasn't going to be ever a home, and such solutions as a home substitute no longer sufficed.

Home is made by the spirit of the people who share it – and she needed a kindred spirit. The nuances within of what constituted akin meant a gigantic difference to her. She quit explaining herself a long time ago, her moves and motives for them. She no longer wrote birthday cards out of politeness, or on time to the people she cared about. She often felt she was prevented from planning her own life, unable to follow a path filled with satisfying work – not a drudgery just to survive.

Karla reflected upon all her jobs that she ever made living with, trying to make sense to herself, and she couldn't – so how to package any of this for sale to others, and mainly – why? Just because many people passing through her life seemed to adopt an attitude of knowing it all, having ideas about how she should live, what she should and could do to improve her lifestyle, and even volunteering their opinions about what she should feel, whom to love, who should and shouldn't be in her life.

All of Karla's steps aiming to improve her situation seemed like under a spell, leading to nowhere. And still, she wasn't willing to give up.

How to get hold of own life? It was slipping through her attempts to make living, as though she lost her way, couldn't find her path, or her path got buried, or perhaps even stolen if something like that was possible, and less and less space, and important people to be with remained.

The people Karla was meeting through her several jobs

showed only interest in taking, as if they were eating her live. For example in the classes she was teaching: after each run they all disappeared without a trace. Did they all run away, because of having caught a glimpse of the true selves in a mirror?

The men who tried to speak to her, oddly enough all gigantic and very tall, were only superficially interested in dating, and mainly in presenting themselves. She just helplessly watched and listened, and finally each time lost patience, hearing about how much they were interesting. Childish men presenting themselves as colorful and entertaining! Silence terrified them.

Perhaps they kept repeating rather habitually their previous successful techniques, believing rubbish about women. Were they hoping to get further with her than with others before? Where to? Certainly not to build any meaningful relationship!

A simple friendship would be nice… Some of them had a wife waiting for them at home, or another significant woman in life, it usually turned out. They would invite her nevertheless for a dinner, and offered a ride home. Maybe they needed fresh air in a good company?

Perhaps she didn't help them with the conversation, and wasn't disclosing her feelings about deeper layers of more meaningful and important areas of life; unskilled in small talk and dating techniques, too childlike, and made of a too foreign matter for them to connect with, and them really being blind, lazy to approach her as they should: a mystery being with an enormous light inside. That's who we all are, no?

To become a supply of a female body, and fill the demand for their *aggrandizement,* or entertain their vague loneliness just didn't suit her.

She knew suddenly – she needed to find herself, she was lost, and these men, unknowingly perhaps, just like the giant landlord, pushed her even further astray by being the wrong company. Could it be that she has tried to live and establish herself in the wrong place, wrong town?

And just like those first settlers who dug a hole in the ground before the winter arrived to survive it, she went to search in her heart. Where was her joy? Why was she on such a lonesome path? Even with friends, Karla usually walked the majority of the steps of the way, or kept on contacting them herself to continue their relationship.

She believed all the people who loved her thought about her often, as she did. She didn't think love should be a chore. It's just there, like music. All one needs to do is hear it. Listen to it. Love depends on life, so we need to live to love! Life depends on love. That was her conclusion.

Refreshed, Karla got up. The day was over and done with its light effects. Time to divert oneself from indulging in a philosophical meditation certainly good for checking in, and get ready to face the evening and night – by herself!

The house was beginning to be crowded with people arriving in from all over the place, and brought from the airport many times a day. Karla lost count of them in the afternoon.

Stomping and door slamming in the hallway, and lots of cell-phone ringing prevented her from any concentrated work. Giggling and the deep voices belonging to invisible giants imposed their volume right behind her door. When Karla opened it, a toddler's face seemed to hang from the ceiling at six-some feet height, greeting her with a sound bass-baritone.

The landlady's cheeks got rosy as she rushed downstairs around the kitchen, smiling. Instead of a nice, sautéed dinner

Karla retrieved own cheese, luckily found in the refrigerator, and climbed fast the three stories back upstairs to gobble it down.

"Cela ne marche pas," she told herself.

One of the trolls took his cell-phone conversation out of the room to the hallway:

"I think I'm old enough to get a tattoo... What kind do you think I should get?... And where on the body...? Oh, hahaha, that must hurt!... How about a skull?!"

Cela ne marche pas! Karla's mind exclaimed loudly. Fortunately, the conversation moved one flight down. From the mix of the voices, the landlady's invitation to the table was singled out:

"Wash your hands, take your shoes off, I just cleaned all rugs and carpets," and the noise shifted downstairs to the dining room.

Karla picked up the phone, hoping to reach someone to talk to. The answering machine began to ring, but Karla didn't feel like leaving a message, yet hanging up seemed even less civil. Reluctantly, she asked for a return call.

It came almost immediately. Would she enjoy staying for a couple of weeks at their house? They'll travel, and Karla might have a pleasant house sitting assignment. When? Well, the day after tomorrow. Would that suit her? She heard hope in their voice. Perhaps their trip came suddenly, and she was the only help they could think of knowing Karla might be alone for Christmas. Would she come over? She'd see them tomorrow.

Peaceful, but temporary; from the mire to a puddle, Karla said to herself. Another empty nest in which she'll try to exist as creatively as possible. Changing things – even if that meant planning on another difficult, but hopeful move.

5

LADY IN A CAP

It was cold but not that cold, rather windy. Some wore hats. Hats set deeply in faces don't necessarily mean cold, or windy. Collars turned up high also don't mean always the chilly wind sneaking through the gaps of our clothes to our spine. Other invisible things running up and down our spine can make us shiver. We hide, hide in the lifted collar, and in hats pulled deep over our face.

She could have warmed up by now already sitting in the plastic shell-seat of a streetcar before I got on, yet her collar was raised, her tweed cap was deeply set in her face, and not even the reflection in the dark streetcar window revealed her features. She sat motionlessly, as though she forgot where she was, or didn't care how far the streetcar would take her.

I guessed her age by the color of her hair, the little of it I could see. A small bun of her blondish, messy curls indicated thirties. A narrow sliver in my view on her right temple revealed gray hair at the roots, the space between her cheeks and below her eyebrows was wide; her high, smooth cheekbones suggested a younger woman.

Suddenly she raised her arms, and began redoing her disheveled hair with shaky fingers of bright reddish, almost orange, or carrot color. The movements were quick, firm, quite anxious, nervous. The result must have felt much better on the head under her cap, yet if I didn't know of her working on the hairdo that just happened I couldn't tell the difference.

All of a sudden she turned her head to the opposite direction. I followed her destination with my eyes. A couple was sitting there embraced lightly, as couples do on Friday night out. Their conversation wasn't audible, but by their listening to one another an air of harmony rippled from them, a sense of familiarity, and peace. Their jackets were undone. The heat inside the streetcar was sufficient to warm up people during the short ride between two stops. The tweed cap woman was staring at the couple without blinking, feeding on their peaceful, quiet exchange.

She was quite handsome, and her light make up suggested that she too was up to something this Friday night. Her eyes, she couldn't take off of the couple, spoke of her loneliness, deep yearning. I was unable to name the color of her eyes, but I could read in them her life experience, not so much youth in the fine wrinkles around her widely opened eyes. She was really beautiful in her thoughtfulness.

Then with a light, long sigh she tilted her head toward the reflective dark window behind which there was a slowly moving, dimly lit downtown street, lined with a row of boutique stores, some still decorated with St. Valentine's hearts and chocolates.

The woman kept on glancing at the couple, for the first

time blinking rapidly, as if sudden tears should be prevented from leaping out. Her head turned back to the window. It was impossible to guess whether she had registered the passing St. Valentine's festive windows.

The couple got off without being noticed by her. After the next turn the tram makes a loop, and goes back to town around the hospital. I was getting off right before the turn to my new temporary place. If she was going to the hospital, one would expect her to carry a bouquet, no? Her arms were empty.

Sometimes we have nothing to carry, the lighter the better. Ladies resemble more ladies when they carry a handbag, a purse of some sort even with wearing jeans and sneakers. It feels less lost. It feels like one has a home where one hangs a purse, in a closet perhaps, or drops it on the floor by the doorway. She was empty-handed.

'Trade comfort for vitality' I read somewhere, go light-weight. I always carried only essentials as if I was on the road, or visiting, but my purse was always packed. Mostly, I felt like I was visiting. What does one need in the purse that can't be stuffed in the pockets? Keys, money, or plastic, a comb, an ID, a phone. That's what a man might need. A lady is expected to have in her purse a lipstick.

This one was empty-handed. She looked calm; her head movements weren't abrupt, but her carrot-colored hands fingering through her loosened hairdo and retightening it spoke of her buried feelings.

People in this country keep their feelings on public to themselves; if anybody notices, or asks: 'How are you today?' they immediately launch a social small talk to dilute imposition, and erase their emotions, or at least neutralize them.

Not connecting the dots, as if life was an isolated

incident, and history something written in the textbooks which reflected none of the subsequent events. What one learns in school then – if anything – is often completely useless for life.

For example, one can't really show off with the historical fact that the Sephardic Jews were expelled from Spain in the same year Columbus put his foot on this land. What's the significance of this? Is that connecting dots?

What one wants are little jewels to shine in a conversation, one needs what stands out, but not too far: a clever collection of pre-chewed, popular, not much controversial topics, quick-picked from the television, or casual conversations, the topics which most of the people agree upon. One is in. No one wants to be singled out.

Single! She must be single! She was lonely, she may have gone to or from an event, hoping to leave with someone, and it just didn't work out. The lady in the cap. She didn't even seem to care if anyone was paying attention to her. Perhaps she thought she was so insignificant that she was almost invisible, who would land an eye on her?

I brought myself back inside the streetcar. Someone could be easily staring at me staring at someone who was staring at people, who didn't care that they were being stared at. Did that happen to be own projection of my escaped, unsettling thoughts, mirroring my own visible reality?

Reality? What reality!? Visible to those who knew me? Who were they? I doubted anyone had a clue. Most of the time the reality felt like a movie someone mad had decided to make, and wherever I went, the people on the streets, or just about anywhere were extras not living a real life, but instructed to begin with pretending of life on 'action!' as soon as I turned a corner.

'Know Thyself.' That is the invisible reality unknown to

most, including myself. If we were honest, we would admit to it. And we would try to find ourselves.

That's why I was watching others when they forgot about themselves, that's why I often randomly pulled off a book from a shelf, and opened it, that's why I paid attention to cats how they monitor our human feelings, because it informed me best. And tranquility.

What if what I see happens because of what I feel? What if my emotions materialize themselves in what's happening within my sight? There are symbols, and there are signs. That would be a great gift, and I would have to treasure it very responsibly. Maybe it's the very symptom of life which is a gift and miracle by itself, and we don't enjoy it, don't approach it with gratitude as an act of love for which we need to give love back.

Perhaps it's too late to understand it, being so advanced in life, already so much has passed by that cannot be reversed. But at least I could agree upon one thing: whenever I found myself on a cross road, I chose the best I could as to which way to go, based on what I knew at the time.

Isn't it odd that people who sound very persuasive are often the biggest liars? And those who speak less and quietly speak the truth? Masters of propaganda; many people vote for the loud ones, only later wondering why things go wrong.

The rain comes down, and the sun shines once in a while at the same time, and the world is preferably colorful. Not this Friday night.

I almost missed my stop, and also didn't notice the lady in the cap getting off. She wasn't at her window; her shell-seat was empty when I left.

The wind outside surprised me with its sweeping

strength. It slowed down my walk. I was left pondering that I might never see the lady in the cap again. I'd never find out what was on her mind which had revealed so much anxiety.

Most probably, it would have never occurred to her that someone was reading her hands while she was fixing her hair. And I was so absorbed in watching her hands that if there was someone watching me, I wouldn't know. And I wouldn't know whether she was headed for a visit in one of the hospitals, or to a date in a bar for a beer and a pool tournament with her carrot colored hands. Or both.

I lifted the collar of my black coat, and struggled to adjust to the cold. Once I did, I was happy to wrestle with the wind blows, and walked briskly all the way home, preparing myself again for another adjustment in temperature: a cold house.

My housemates agreed upon energy preservation to an absurd degree, keeping the house so cold that even cooking required wearing a coat. This consensus for the common areas in this beautiful, but drafty old house prompted me to bring in my private room an oil space heater, and hibernate there most of the time.

The house cats quickly realized my room was the coziest, warmest in the house, and visited me nightly. They crawled together in my bed, shifting accordingly with my changing positions.

They both, being a long time housemates, had a peculiar way of treating each other, sometimes quietly disagreeing, sometimes licking each other's faces vehemently, and then swirling into one warm, hairy ball, only peeking at me when I was about to sit next to them, while taking my clothes off; one cat with blue, one with golden eyes.

It was the most representative image of a home. Symbolic. In the golden light of one evening, I caught their mutual washing each other on my camcorder. My home soon will be packed away again, and moved somewhere else. How many more times? As if all this time I was being trained in non-attachment.

Perhaps that's why people like to own dogs, because dogs get attached to their master, and give the satisfaction, or an illusion of obedience. The humans then can fulfill their need for something, or someone they can control.

The cats can't really be controlled. They remain mysterious, and logical by their own design, on their own terms. They appear independent, but in fact, they are very loyal, and grateful. If they are hungry, of course, they beg for food, and they shouldn't have to – their metabolism works differently. Dogs can be fed just once a day, on the other hand. So, I ended up feeding the cats secretly whenever they asked. Maybe that was why they kept on coming to my quarters – bonding over the food, or over my understanding of their needs. Maybe they knew mine.

Even though they weighed heavy on my feet, I slept better, deeper. My nights were always more peaceful when some other breathing being shared my space with me. Except for the time when I was married. The bedroom then represented the least desired place at home. I never looked forward to go to bed, never slept well there, never felt private, loved, respected. A huge misunderstanding. The substance was missing – the spirit, the love. Once the trust was broken, it couldn't be restored. The safety was gone. One often chooses rather facing the fate alone. At least for some time.

As I walked past the busy streets toward the residential area with old homes, the clamor of the traffic subsided, the cold wind in the leafless branches caused my steps to compensate for the blows and soon, they absorbed all audible sounds.

One could see the inhabitants cooking their dinner in the softly lit windows, or resting on a sofa in front of a TV set, or working on a computer, with their faces illuminated by the blue screen. All looked single. Were they? Of course not, but it seemed like it.

These brief revelations stayed frozen in the mind as a still life. Assumptions framed them as pictures of what someone else's life might be like. The flashes of understanding, and then, the light was turned off.

Our house was lit brighter than usually, and when I unlocked, both cats rushed out.

A pleasant cooking smell and warmth followed the cats outside through the doorway. A cheerful voice caught up with me, as I was ascending the creaking steps:

"You are welcome to join the dinner party!"

"Thank you, I'll be down in a minute!"

The heat was on! Exception to the thrifty rule for the guests to enjoy the party.

In the hallway, I glanced at myself in the mirror, usually comforted by the sight. The indirect, soft light reflected my features quite mercifully. I could fool myself into the notion that this was how everyone else perceived me: younger, examining, soulful – that was what I usually caught in the mirror.

I wondered if what I saw was a glimpse of substance, or a rare appearance, or if – like that lady in the cap – I also forgot myself, and projected an image which might, or might not be seen as reflected in the mirror, and it wasn't how people perceived me.

The large, rectangular table in the dining room

downstairs was set, extended for extra seating. The light blue table cloth with tiny flower pattern, fresh flowers scattered all over it, wine, silverware, matching candles, but every chair came from a different set, the whole feel was very festive, and reminded me of my teens, and the unusual household I had lived in then, being the only one of that age, and feeling often misunderstood, burdensome to all, except for my three years old sister.

My housemates were present, and several guests already as well. I happened to know a few of them. Everyone brought a dish but me who didn't know about the good bye party.

Introduction to those I didn't know was brief, and to my delight, people spoke in various accents of English.

"Yes, I am European too. I teach history classes in one of the colleges in town, no future in it, barely making a living, it has never been easy in this town, but San Francisco which I love, and where I've lived for years, has got so expensive."

"We couldn't afford to buy a house there."

"My wife also teaches."

"Well, the way the things are going I'm worried that in ten to twenty years I'll be a bag lady eating cat food," the wife added with a tired smile.

"So, let's enjoy what we've got today on the menu, shall we?" said another dinner companion whose legs stretched all the way underneath the table, so that he touched mine. He quickly apologized with a gracious gesture. Not an American, I assumed. None of these couples had the neurotic need to demonstrate their bond in front of me, a single person, no one was that insecure. What a pleasure.

I began to thaw, mellowed more by the great red wine, chosen with thought and finesse to accompany the eclectic meatless dishes.

"No, I don't come from a Sephardic family. My family came the other way."

"So did mine."

How odd, I was just thinking a while ago about the 1492 year when the Sephardic Jews were expelled from Spain, and when Columbus discovered America.

"Isn't the whole world in a mass exodus? Which reminds me of a good anecdote about choosing a country to immigrate to."

"Yes, there's no country one would pick today, is it?" said one of the wives.

"Yes," I spoke out, finally, "we would need a whole new globe."

Several heads looked at me with a silent question.

"That's what Roubitchek asked for at the immigration office," answered instead of me the dinner companion with the long legs. Quite a European style!

The heads smiled, reconstructing the joke in their thoughts, filling the blanks. I was wondering if fear, or at least caution, would prevent people from telling a joke like this, just like I remembered from the dark times I had lived through back 'home'.

Maybe no one felt like joking, too close to home, perhaps jokes were becoming something rather obscene in the times of war. Maybe these good, educated people thought in a similar way, as immigrants, knowing much about fears of losing a job, the careful political correctness, eavesdropping, suspicions, were noticing how a green card wasn't really a very protecting status; at least their children were born here, fortunately. Was that a fortune?

"Well, I was born here, and I wish I wasn't, I feel a lot of shame."

We all lifted our heads from our delicious food, and examined my housemate whose parents owned the house.

"That's unnecessary, that's far fetched," I heard myself saying.

"But I do."

"I feel pain for this country too," I continued. "It has always been a dream democracy to most of the oppressed people behind the Iron Curtain."

I could see how the debate might turn passionate before I finished my train of thoughts. I hurried:

"Despite events of infuriating injustice, racism violently expressed, ugly wars, and all, we looked up to it; and now the dream has become a nightmare from which we all are waking up, crying like little babies. But I still love this country."

A ponderous silence filled the room. I wasn't finished, but felt that with the next expressed thought they would look at me like I was mad.

"I think we still need to be grateful for the opportunity to learn, not to despair – which happens to be a vice. "

"Faith, we need faith."

Surprisingly, the dinner companion who had edited the immigration joke said this.

"Where would you go get it? To the church?"

"No. It's a gift. Like life is. One needs to treat it so. Precious. It's there, here. Look at this flower." He picked up a tired rose.

"Doesn't it revive your faith?"

Oh, someone was as mad as myself, but compared to me he's got guts to speak up.

My shame-stricken housemate got up, and put on music. She couldn't take the emotional burden anymore. What an extraordinary evening! I haven't spoken to people who feel, think, speak, study, share food, thoughts, feelings for so long!

The soft music was unknown to me, not striking enough,

but not obnoxious; I was unable to determine its style, or the country by the rhythm, or by the instruments, until the singer began whisper the lyrics. Russian. I recognized the singer: Alla Pugacheva.

I immediately recalled a situation almost 20 years old. I was employed as a maid in a hotel where many immigrants worked in low-skilled jobs, fresh in the country, and often not speaking any English. It was before the Berlin Wall fell.

One day I was sent to clean a master suite on the top floor. The only cleaning needed there was to vacuum, and empty the trash can. On the bottom of the waste basket, there were a few department store receipts, and tags torn off the new clothes. All of a sudden, a young man entered from the bedroom, while I was dragging the heavy vacuum cleaner in. He acknowledged my presence as he would notice a fly on the wall, and spoke in Russian through the crack of the bedroom door over his shoulder, addressing someone by the name of Alla.

"I'll wait for you in the bar, hurry up."
He was wearing a brand new black leather jacket. The female voice answered something in a whiny, spoiled way. It was the famous Soviet pop star Alla Pugacheva, touring the United States.
I felt deeply humiliated in my terrible uniform, being just a maid to someone who could freely travel, and represent the Soviet 'best of the best'. I had plenty of time for the rest of the day to sort this experience out. I used the conclusion as a propeller to learn English as fast as possible, and really well.

"How long ago have you arrived to this country, dear? More wine?"
Everyone quieted down, and was now waiting for my answer.

"I still have some, thanks. It'll be twenty years soon, for me and my kids."

"You speak well, and almost with no accent."

"Funny you say so, I was just thinking about the people who told me about my accent twenty years ago, and I didn't speak well at all then. Just recently I was told here in town that my slight accent might be an obstacle in getting work."

"Well," interjected my shame-stricken housemate, "it's really hard to make a living as an artist in this country... Don't even go there!" She sounded harsh.

"That's why I teach, and that's why I keep writing."

I wouldn't complain. I chose my path a long time ago. Maybe the path chose me. But people tend to forget that in the times of war the Muses keep silent. Not that the Muses wouldn't try, but people become less perceptive from anxiety, and more disconnected. The audience tend to deliberately escape from the reality into realms that provide them with no confrontation. Art gets to us on its own terms, fortunately.

"And what do you teach, dear?"

The long-legged guest with a pleasant British accent filled my glass again with the cheerful red wine.

"My native language, and my own course I've designed... For personal development, for creativity, for inspiration."

"Is that an art therapy course?" asked my other housemate who lived across the hallway – without curiosity, grinning politely.

"No, not really. More transforming."

His girlfriend began giggling:

"Some New Age stuff?"

"No, no one's doing this, it's my idea of employing my professional and life experiences, and give people tools to grow, dream; they really usually go after their dreams, when they graduate."

"Neat. Know Thyself. Cheers!" clinked with me the long-legged dinner guest.

The giggling girlfriend, the youngest of all of us, blinked her eyes a few times, until she attracted everyone's attention, and asked:

"Have you, guys, seen 'The Secret'? I think it's awesome. Not that I am into the New Age stuff."

A smaller group of the dinner guests appreciated the lighter note, and began joking and bashing the film.

The history professor and his Israeli fellow professor moved their chairs closer to the other end of the big, still quite festive looking dining table with flickering candles. The history professor approached me:

"I am about to teach my students a chapter on Cold War. Would you be interested in coming to my class, and telling the students your own story?"

How odd, I thought, all these incidents lined up! I had to laugh:

"Do you hear the music? It's Russian, Soviet!"

The Israeli professor acknowledged the ownership of the tape, and mentioned his interest in 'obscure music', as he called this tape a rarity.

"Well, she used to be really famous in her country."

I couldn't avoid sharing my refreshed memory of cleaning her suite, including my resolve to learn English well. Some eyebrows rose in surprise, not due the coincidence of the obscure music, but due my first official, and unenviable job in the United States of America which was the only time my kids and I had any medical insurance.

I promised to come to the history class.

As I was thinking of what to tell the students to help them in relating to such a remote experience, I traveled in time to my grandfathers. They could be my starting points.

One was drafted in the First World War as an accountant in the Czechoslovak Legions that went to fight in Russia on the Eastern Front, still under the Austro-Hungarian Empire, all the way to Vladivostok, while my grandmother was waiting for him for 7 years to come back.

My other grandfather in his youthful excitement, at the time a teenager, became a founding member of the Communist Party after the Austro-Hungarian Empire disintegrated. His communist indoctrination of 'the class hatred' must have begun some times then.

In the same year, 1921, my maternal grandfather returned from the First World War through Siberia, long ways form home.

It occurred to me, they would have been enemies, and if the time, and opportunity favored it – and of course, neither of them ever fired a gun at a person – but in theory, they would have been shooting at each other from the opposite side of a barricade.

The hero legionary came back with broken health; his second peptic ulcer surgery a few years later was fatal. My grandmother – whom I never met either – lived only two years longer than her beloved husband. My mom, at age four and then six, along with her older brother orphaned, after their mom, my grandmother, passed away. Thank goodness, their great-aunt Albina, a retired girls' school principal, sixty five years old, took both children into her care.

During the Second World War they lived in Pilsen, the town later liberated by the Americans within the demarcation line. But that fact was erased from the history textbooks when I was growing up; the Soviet Red Army was the only recognized celebrated liberator. It was dangerous to even mention otherwise, however vividly was the end of the Second World War remembered by many.

The other grandfather was obviously imprisoned during the war, and survived the concentration camps Buchenwald, and Dachau, curiously enough liberated by the Americans as well.

His son, my father, idealized him as a hero, seeing him as a thirteen years old boy behind bars: a political prisoner jailed by the Germans in occupied Prague. With his grandmother, they'd visit the famous Pankrác prison to bring him food in a bundle. It must have marked my father for life.

As if my birth, my existence, was a symbol of that Big Split between true and false which both of my grandfathers represented in their paths, of course, I was learning those facts much later. Perhaps, my birth and life could also symbolically heal the Big Split, bring to light the truth?

We all got profoundly shaken by the wars, including the Cold War. Our lives got shattered, got rolled over by the Warsaw Pact Armies, 30 divisions of the 'Brotherly Armies' on August 21st, 1968, and both nations, the Czechs and Slovaks, got decimated with 'just a few victims' losing their lives, 'just a few drops of spilled blood', but utterly decimated spiritually, economically, culturally, and mainly morally.

Has anyone ever cared for a small nation, except perhaps to sell it? And since then – how many more people's lives in how many more lands? We used to firmly believe that the holocaust and the Second World War were so terrible the whole world had learned its lesson, and no Third World War could ever come!

Perhaps, until everyone on this Earth understands we are all connected with one another by the oceans, land, air, seen, and unseen physical, and other forces, and that we all are just guests here, there can't be peace.

So, the dinner party gathered to say good bye to the old house which has provided me with a temporary illusion of home. It will go for sale.

A new search for a place started over again. Phone calls, ads that almost never reflected what was really available, always hiding something, like a mad dog, or a crazy dog owner, or loud, disobedient children – 'You must love children'.

'No more pets' meant usually 7 live cats and 25 cats buried in the 'large backyard'; 'green thumb' suggested someone mowing their lawn at six in the morning on Sunday under your window; 'an occasional party' gave the chance to hope for a good night sleep once a month, when everyone went to party someplace else.

I found a couple whose three children fled home to the college, and the couple was searching for 'a teacher' to rent a room to in their house.

"You said you were from Yugoslavia?" inquired the potential landlord. "Well, how about you stop by on Saturday. Friday I am busy dissecting an octopus." Well, maybe I won't stop by even on Sunday...

This town has been so uneasy; did I want to trap myself in a twelve-month lease? What if my situation evolves so dramatically I'd need to break it? I kept on scrolling down the craigslist section 'For Rent', my eyes already tired. These conditions always somewhat scared me.

Not that I would desire a house, feeling settled, however I wished for bringing all of my scattered possessions from around the world into one nest: photos, diaries, old silverware, china, grandmother's table cloths, pictures on the walls, letters, notes, my ancient record collection – if it all still exists, and mainly my dear books.

I've always wanted a piano. When I was young, we always had one at home: now I couldn't have one because of constant moving. I've always loved having people visiting, and liked to host cool, improvised events in my house; I'd love to set my house so that I'd use a large room as a studio, empty space more or less – for concerts, little shows, readings, a changeable space. Then instead of me moving, everything would be coming my way.

There must be a place for me; a suitable place for me... Maybe not in this town? My financial situation too has been beyond calling it poor. Practically, I was homeless. No matter what I'd tried in this town to make a living, everything had disintegrated. Nothing seemed to last more than a few months. Was it the general struggle of an immigrant whose coming and staying in this country has become increasingly more difficult and complicated since 'the war on terror' began? Was it every immigrant's story? I doubted it.

Translators, interpreters, subtitling, a little better paid language assignments with the knowledge of technical aspects involving computers could perhaps open a new field? My country men and women surely already grabbed all of those jobs.

Most of the time, I didn't do well near my countrymen. I've evolved more likely into an international citizen, and found the typical reactions of my countrymen strange, remotely reminding me of the past life in a culture where it was common to first tell a lie instead of the truth, because telling the truth made one too vulnerable.

This mode of thinking often immigrated with the people to the new country as well; when the misrepresentation of the truth got confronted in the new cultural context, when a lie was found out, the most common reaction of a countryman was ranging from irritation to anger and cynicism, assuming the cynicism a valid platform which we, 'all good countrymen', would agree upon, and could endlessly and happily complain to one another, meeting up for 'a beer and a chat' – a gossip – occasionally, until it felt home, bashing together everything too big in the new country, including potatoes.

I put aside the memories of how we used to struggle in the old country to walk with our chins up, how I always carefully watched over my young children, so they wouldn't get infected by the oppressive fear at schools. I had developed a warning red light against the double standards, and brainwashing. Fortunately, my mom and my stepfather, who suffered from the regime for being honest, were our stronghold as well.

These memories ushered themselves to the forefront of my thoughts, because the world seemed to have gone backwards in the past seven years, as if back to the years of the Cold War.

Can I explain any of this to the history students who grew up in the world's longest existing democracy with open debates over the essential human rights, needs, and watched or participated in the massive demonstrations against wars, whose parents were exposed to terrible conflicts, assassinations, repressions, racial injustices, hunger, and poverty in the richest country in the world, but who could at least try to do something openly about it?!

Would be these students influenced by their parents' past, like my generation by the inherited burden of the two world wars, carried over to us?

Everyone came to this country as an immigrant, perhaps not everyone wishes to be reminded of it, their identity is now American, and their ancestry a celebrated folklore. Maybe that's why my housemate felt her shame.

What did I feel? Eradicated, homeless, taken advantage of, often being taken for granted, flown around to and fro like a swirl of dry grass. Attempting to connect the dots, unable, and unwilling to deal with fragments. What, and whom did I relate to?

Maybe I related to the lost souls like that lady in the tweed cap the other day on the streetcar, how she was perusing the couple, the two people who had a relationship. To the displaced people, to those who want to learn, who wish to create, who respond to our shaky situation in the unsettled world with love, just about to anyone sensitive, I related easily.

What was that one guest, the architect, at the party saying about the hippest home design in California these days? It was deliberately designed with regards to the separate lives in the household, for people not to having to see each other for days. The special feature was 'a double master bedroom' with a split bed by a wall. The wife doesn't have to listen to her snoring husband, and he can't complain she stole his comforter. Comforting?

And what means my trotting to and fro? My trying to re-connect, my attempts to find the soil where I could down-root again, transplant, add layers, with many soulful connections underneath? Maybe among those are the sounds of my mother tongue, the Slavic diminutives of which for example Russian is full. It makes the language so feminine, English doesn't have that. What was so moving me to tears in that old Russian film I watched the other day? The language, or something from my childhood my soul recognized?

A pair of little boots I used to wear in winter with the metallic tiny horseshoes that made my every step distinctly ring when I ran back and forth to the ice-skating rink ahead of my great-grand aunt Albina, who was not only a stand-in as my grandmother, but who also taught me about the power of love, and magic of delight, who was lagging behind on two canes, who was eighty four then?

Was it the female character in that film that had reminded me of her? Or another character quoting Pushkin which always profoundly touched my heart?

Was it the director's painful love with which he prostrated a homage to his fatherland, his people, the ancestors, family, his awe at the quiet heroism, the invisible women's deeds, who carried the nation's burden on their shoulders, raising children, grandchildren alone, as it's still true today?

Was it my regret that there had been so few personal accounts like this, addressing the matters in Czechoslovakia which no longer existed as such? Was it my trying to answer why with just a vague answer, naming it due the insufficiently descriptive words the lack of national self-understanding, including history, seeming so negligible in the world's current huge, global issues, and still being able to proudly say I was Czech?

But hasn't this rather become a worldwide trend? Wiping out identities? Nation's histories by re-writing individual lives as it pleased those who wished to leave their marks undisturbed by wrinkles, left by people like myself?

Was it perhaps the sound of poetry in Russian, read by an outstanding actor reminding me of the decades of danger that certain poetry posed to Stalin which only could be whispered, passed on verse by verse, like in the old times before the invention of the press around 1440? People had to remember everything, memorize everything, writing things down was impossible, dangerous to the writer, and the author alike, and also to the messenger. Almost the whole nation in dissent.

Voluntarily or not. Consciously or not.

Many names won't be remembered, never recognized, people have perished without a trace. The film told about this in fragments, the way soul remembers and mirrors itself in dreams.

Perhaps for me it was that quiet, and insisting tone of voice the film used. Closer to the Czech way, downplayed, which unfortunately is neither deep nor peak in emotions, as it's manifested in the Russian nature, and some other, more passionate Slavs, the Serbs for instance, so cursed, because of the Balkan war.

But how to responsibly give an account of what I believed the students should hear from me as 'my personal story', and squeeze it in one hour?

A phone call from the history professor came a few days before my class visit with a program proposal, and included an invitation to a quick dinner, and a surprise film projection during the class. That'll fill up the class, I thought, and perhaps my editing of 'my personal story' to a shorter version would make it stronger.

The school address was very close to mine, and the brief dinner in a walking distance from it. It was dark already and rainy; on the corner, we picked up the film in a rental place that carried lots of foreign films; I was intrigued by the interesting selection and the owner's good taste. The trip to the movie store toured my extended neighborhood, and I could imagine if I lived there, and taught at least part time long term, I could call it almost home.

To dine with a relaxed, knowledgeable, unpretentious, witty, and intelligent man was a treat. The innuendos were naturally excluded, for our social interactions have originated in Europe, and were almost subconsciously imbedded in the same generation.

Even when he behaved chivalrously – opening the door for me, and pulling my chosen chair at a table out and in, a common courtesy when I was growing up, and I responded with happy smiles – it all meant just a pleasant, civil, and cultured exchange that I'd realized was disappearing from my daily life. I appreciated tremendously the ease of the evening so far, regardless of my self-consciousness: my speech was still ahead of me.

I got never used to business lunches, or dinners in America. I could either eat, or seriously concentrate on a conversation, yet our talk went smoothly, and the delicious food accompanied the dialogue naturally, as if we had been long time friends.

The classroom was empty when the professor set up for the movie projection as the first part of the session. He didn't tell me anything about it, except that it was a 1968 documentary.

I sat down and watched the students rushing in, mostly adults with sympathetic features who took the history class in addition to their technical degree.

One woman began to nervously retie her hair, and I – in disbelief how the world was small – searched with my eyes for the tweed cap in all possible places, like her pockets, her purse – which she didn't have the other night on the tram. Finally, relieved, I spotted her tweed cap sitting on her shopping bag.

The professor reiterated the tonight's class program, introduced the visitor, me, and finally turned the lights off. We got to watch the surprise movie.

I was immediately struck by the feelings at home: the

film was a short series of documents made for the Czechoslovak Television during the week of August 18, 1968, day by day: pictures from the sleepy, familiar towns showing vacationers, and spa guests attending a fashion show, until the current news mentioned the government and the increasingly adverse reactions of the Warsaw Pact to the culminating political development in Czechoslovakia which started with 'the Prague Spring'; the meeting of the officials in a border town on the train tracks in a wagon kept secret; a few government members were held hostage, I recalled what at the time we heard 'between the lines'.

The whole river of recollections overwhelmed me with emotions deeply rooted in my identity; and I couldn't stop the tears coming out, obstructing my watching. I was trying not to sob loudly, and keep on watching.

The filmmakers' emotions also tinted the shots: how to stay neutral when you were learning about your own government's communiqué which in brief revealed its fear, and willingness to succumb to the pressure from the Soviets? The old images stirred my heart.

The next short document made for the television by the same crew captured the Soviet tanks rolling over the bridge, leading to the governmental offices on the banks of the Vltava River. The astonished film crew was passing the tanks in the opposite direction, headed early morning for an assignment out of town which obviously at this point couldn't happen.

The commenting narration in Czech explained the film crew's experiences, subtitled below in a very short English version, probably added in a hurry later. This film was never shown in Czechoslovakia, I realized, it must have been absolutely banned, and later smuggled out of the country, but its existence must have been well known to the authorities who sought for it vehemently, including the documentarists, for destruction and punishment.

The crew continued to film all the events in Prague from Day 1 of the occupation, mostly from hidden positions.

The footage from Prague of the peaceful, quite heroic uprising of the citizens; their talking in Russian to the Soviet soldiers, asking them why they came, and explaining to them there was no 'contra-revolution' to suppress. The faces of young soldiers who in the state of shock – ready to shoot and kill an enemy – listened to the Russian speaking, concerned, civilized people.

The footage with the Soviet tanks, aiming at the Prague Radio Broadcast building also documented its shelling, and setting the building on fire, its hasty evacuation; the news broadcast from undisclosed locations, often in people's basements; students' organized demonstrations; and lots of heroic acts of the regular men and women who tried helping to keep the country in own people's hands, while the government was held under a siege for days, without any news, or connection to the nation, and was constantly pressured by the Soviets.

The huge manifestation in the center of Prague where I recognized the young faces of a few friends in the front rows reminded me how young we were then.

My own recollection of my whereabouts in those days ran through my head simultaneously: the invasion news caught up with us in Yugoslavia during the summer vacation, celebrating with my mom's family my high school graduation.

The details of that terribly sad time were still alive in my mind: the local boys compassionately comforting me, taking me for long walks along highways; and when a colon of trucks full of armed young men, ready to help fighting against the invasion headed to the borders, the boys would wave, and point at me, calling out: 'She's Czech!' The rifles in the young men's hands would raise, and I was passionately saluted by the armed volunteers, my Slavic brothers, from the passing trucks.

The shock of the invasion led to the necessity of considering the available options for our bleak future prospects, inevitably and completely shattered which we could only intuitively perceive at the time; but we still hoped for an open world, the possibility to travel, and study abroad.

We couldn't imagine the damage on the spirit, culture, moral integrity, the loss of the basic liberties, and of course, the unbearable economic situation, sanctions, and retributions of the toughened regime, wide spread corruption, forced and willing collaborations with the totalitarian regime, the censorship, vicious political persecutions, imprisonments of the dissidents and their families, forced expelling from the country, betrayals, cynicism, and mainly the grip of the crippling fear.

The process was officially known as 'Normalization': every single citizen was urged to call the invasion, and the subsequent occupation a 'brotherly help by the friendly armies against the contra-revolution', and every person was pressured to sign this official statement – or else!
In these ways, among others on the daily basis, the whole nation was taught to shamefully lie, and endorse the lie by own signature. Stigma. Who refused, faced serious consequences.

It was sheer luck I'd never met the challenge of signing any such enforced piece of paper, being without an employer at the crucial times. Other quite risky situations, however, tested my dedication to telling the truth, even when I was really, really afraid.

When the film was over, I walked upfront, and simplified my talk. My emotional reaction to the documentary almost disabled my speech about the life behind the Iron

Curtain, the symbol of Cold War; and I was moved by the students' reaction to the film, and their intelligent questioning.

The lady with the tweed cap raised her hand. I prompted her to speak. Her voice was raspy and accented. I could place it to a Slavic country. She told us she was from Sarajevo, and could completely relate to the film, and my story.

Immediately, I visualized the main boulevard in Sarajevo through which we entered the city in a car with my colleagues, attending a summer festival in 2001, its streets, and buildings, marked with scars of the war, and by the long siege, wide openings with missing houses, burnt high rise apartment blocks, and many, many new cemeteries with countless white crosses for miles and miles, seen while passing through the Serbian, Croatian, and Bosnian countryside which kept us all in the car solemn for hours, until someone began quietly singing.

She reminded me of another associated moment: my speechless experience of standing on the high bank above the green river Neretva in Mostar, the town divided into half Christian, half Muslim, for centuries reconciled by the means of a bridge – *most* – proud, medieval, masoned, famous – now gone, blown up.

I was wandering would I be lucky to find out also about the purpose of the tweed cap lady's travel the other night.

She surely answered my question – in her own way, mentioning her only family member left from fighting the war; arriving to the United States, and his presently undergoing a treatment in a local hospital. She didn't finish her narration; her voice gave up on her.

I thought – there must be such a great, unhealed pain, losses, feelings of homelessness, and uprooted lives... What a bloody century we were all born into! Was it going to change?

The history professor wrapped up the class with words of thanks. The students thoughtfully collected their belongings, marking hopefully this evening as a powerful lesson in history.

And for me, I received more than I gave, I found more than I left behind.

6

NO SELF-PITY, NO CRUELTY

She called herself Irish with a lisp caused by her protruding
front teeth from sucking her thumb, still at the age of twelve
during the night. She was tiny, reddish blond, and tough. She
was waiting to be placed in a foster care home as the rest of the
girls at the residence.

A bold sign was attached to her name, alerting all the staff
about her severe allergy to bee sting with a bolder print of the
emergency instructions, in case she encountered one.

Just like the rest of the girls, she already knew the
system, and how to ride it. Distrustful to all the adults, like the
other girls who regularly flexed their muscles in telling their
life stories, painfully sad, and tragic, who often found pleasure
in competing whose horrors were more sorrowful: how many
times they ran away, where did they end up when caught,
which drugs they tried, and how many boyfriends turned
pimps, this Irish, pale mini-girl never smiled, and seldom

spoke. In place of speaking she'd dress up. T-shirts with signs, green color was often her choice, hand made bracelets, anklets, simple hair ornaments. Silent messages. Still playful in her solitary way of an abandoned child.

She was struggling with reading out loud when it was her turn in taking over the next chapter of a passed around book, yet she seemed to enjoy reading a library book of her choice, crouching in the corner by a large window which allowed a little more daylight, sifted through the thickness of unkept bushes and trees.

The windows, firmly fastened, wouldn't open, and all the doors, including the refrigerator, cupboards, and drawers were locked up.

'No self-pity and no cruelty' say the Irish is their credo. The girl only had a vague sense of the place called Ireland on the globe, and except of overhearing somewhere that the Irish were excellent ball players, all of her Irishness was resting in her stubborn determination to go there one day. One day. We all have our dreams to survive traumas.

One early summer day, there came a disruption of an otherwise routine regimen, and it was promising to continue weekly all summer long. The program director agreed to an hour of a theater class offered by a real actress!

"Anything for those girls... helps! Wednesdays will work."

The actress was briefed about the individual cases upon her request through reading the admission log. One entry stated:

'Mom refuses to allow child come home. Child didn't do well at... because she's Muslim and they are Christian based. Client has possible suicide attempts, in the past she tried to jump off a balcony and then threatened her mother with a knife, and then tried to use the knife on herself... Her mother doesn't speak well English and the child reports that she has mental issues. The mom fled Somalia and went to Kenya after witnessing her husband being murdered while she was pregnant with the child...'

The first theater session was meshed with curiosity from the girls and staff alike who were casing out the 'real actress' and her games on that rainy afternoon.

The second session got interrupted manifold by family visits scheduled curiously for the same time, the staff's loud fussing about, and by the admission of a new child who immediately retired on her bed, coughing, and feverishly drinking cold water, claiming she was not feeling well.

For the third time the actress asked for the permission to take the group of seven girls for a stroll in the neighborhood. The permission was granted. With one only coughing girl left behind the staff would gain an hour of peace.

The girls got excited by the prospect of leaving the gloomy premises, painted a long time ago in green and blue on very dilapidated walls. They couldn't wait to 'check out the rich houses'. Their temporary residence, tucked as a cul-de-sac at the end of a winding road on a hill, was built in the vicinity of spacious, old family houses, but also near new, architect-designed, artful homes, fitted into the steep terrains.

The plan for this third session was a heart opening theme of 'dreams for life', using the exposure to the natural, and created beauty in the urban lifestyle to expand the girls' horizons. Aiming high, perhaps...

Often, the non-material world manifests itself in revealing the substance to a sensitive person. In order to see those interesting buildings, the group needed to find a path in the hillside leading to the street on top of the hill lined with homes on both sides. The Irish girl knew of narrow, steep, old stone stairs with a canopy of honeysuckle, now too late to find it abloom. The girls agreed to climb the steps through the green tunnel.

The view above the stairs opened up to enjoy the cascading gardens on both sides of the wide, sunny street, occupied by many different song birds, and wings flopping, colorful butterflies, gardens in which many more or less artful objects spoke of the owner's taste.

For a while, the girls only wrestled with catching up their breath, being quite out of shape due their confinement, unused to any stretching, or movement. Their renewed conversations abandoned the usual horrific themes, and commented on the present experience, pointing to random homes playfully – 'this one is mine'.

Their cheeks acquired color, one girl was humming a song perhaps unaware of the fact, two girls trotted side by side hooked by their arms, one girl shyly joined the 'real actress', her features softened by the fresh, fragrant air.

The Irish girl lagged last, pondering about something: a deep crease was cutting in the middle of her forehead, her bare shoulders lightly sweat. The actress slowed down to let the Irish girl pass by in front of her. The girl got joined by the wildest, loudest and silliest, dark-haired girl, the youngest of them all. Her eyes quickly leered at the actress, and then she inclined her head to the Irish girl who uttered something quickly into her ear.

It occurred to the actress she had put herself into a very vulnerable position with seven runaway girls. They were not getting any closer back to the residence, the streets followed the terrain horizontally without any crossing path to the lower level of the slope. If the girls decided to take off, there was no way to stop them! The time of the day was conducive, the weather ideal. On the other hand, if they planned to escape, they wouldn't know which way to descend the hill, and would be captured fast.

The actress relaxed, and kept talking to distract the girls' potential thoughts from such ideas, and offered to turn around, laughing about getting lost. Without intentionally scaring her clowning class, she succeeded at their grabbing on her, or staying close. They didn't feel like getting lost.

A U-turn led them along the opposite side of the sunlit street with hanging gardens. Amazed, they sniffed all the varieties of roses for which the city was famous. They entertained themselves by exclaiming the names they either read on the names tags, or heard them clearly pronounced by the actress.

"Gloria Dei! Jericho! Eleanor Roosevelt!"

Some girls got enchanted and inspired so much that they decided to name their future children after the roses. The street turned downhill as if by magic, and allowed the group to find their way to the residence on time without passing through the dark honeysuckle tunnel.

One of the staff members was spotted by the girls at the gate. The woman quickly stomped on her cigarette when she saw the group returning, and rushed back toward the building.

As soon as the group passed through the gate, the Irish girl made a sudden spastic grimace for no apparent reason. Her wild, younger companion smiled, and announced:

"She got stung!"

Where was the bee? What timing!

In a few steps the class reached the locked door of the residence, and the actress rang the bell. The girls looked refreshed, happy.

New staff has arrived for the later shift, and was mingling with the morning counselors. The fresh residential counselors were very tall, distant, icy cold, young women. They dispensed the prescribed tranquilizers with an elevated, unconcerned attitude, quite aware of their intimidating position.

The Irish girl pressed through the group straight to the office with her expressive spastic mask causing the actress to be scolded, while other staff members called 911.

The emergency medical crew arrived in less than five minutes, administered an injection, and plugged her to the oxygen apparatus, as if the girl was already gone. Routine.

Before the Irish girl got strapped to a stretcher, carried out, and shoved inside the ambulance, she gave the actress, crushed by the situation, a mild, victorious smile. Her eyes were already affected by the sting allergy injection. In a few minutes she was going to be rescued from the residence, and catered to in a hospital like a star.

Her wild friend whispered to the actress in the hallway:

"She faked it, she told me. She scratched an old mosquito bite. She just wanted to get out of here… lucky!"

True or false? Freedom is intoxicating.

The truth was that the planned fourth theater session never happened, nor the rest of them, being choked in the heat of the summer by the icy cold, jealous staff, and couldn't be backed up by the well-wishing program director who had abruptly resigned from his job, leaving the wreaking ship to her fate, captain free, as his legacy.

THE PATH

Just for a few minutes, in the shade, in the relative peace I wanted to rest. Until a siren of an ambulance disturbed it, and made me to set aside my pen, and raise my hands to cover my overwhelmed ears.

The ambulance arrived to a near by crosswalk at the next segment of the downtown city park. I continued writing again where I left off: the address on the envelope, exactly on the date of the anniversary of our landing in this country. Very symbolic. Past few days I've been reflecting on all those years.

Another disturbance entered my left ear, and my head followed the noise, my eyes noticing all the people sitting on the benches in the park, or standing in the shade of old, tall trees, under their canopies, or walking, who gradually also directed their heads toward the same place from which the loud voice was coming, exclaiming some words.

A younger looking, unshaved man was rhythmically waving his arm all the way to his face, and kept repeating:

"My body is telling me – Stop thinking, stop thinking, stop thinking!"

Each time he would slap his forehead with the palm of his swinging arm. He passed everyone, but occasionally, he'd briefly stop, and address someone with his repetitive message.

He passed me as well and continued where the paramedics from the ambulance were helping someone who had fallen ill.

I quickly glanced at the young man's expression if it would reveal whether he was a genuine nut, or an actor from the urban liberal arts college next to the park who was going over his lines. He looked too real, too fiercely hitting his head for an actor on his lunch break. His other hand carried an undisturbed smoking cigarette, and sunglasses.

I finally finished my copying the unusual numbers of the address when the young man's voice screamed out in my direction:

"Heart attack! This is a heart attack!"

Then he turned around, and walked back continuing his routine – hitting himself over own forehead:

"My body's asking me: stop thinking, stop thinking, stop thinking…."

I couldn't take the voice anymore, the peacelessness, and got up looking for a post office to send my important mail off. Of course, we bumped into each other with the young, highly disturbed man. His walking loop brought him back again. He stopped, I stopped. His face was full of sweat, and a distant pain, and he seemed trapped in his world.

I made a gesture of a polite yielding, but he stood there like frozen, he couldn't move even one finger as if I completely derailed him. I proceeded past him, and found my way to the empty, marble-and-brass, art déco post office. The clerk asked me as if I was crazy:

"You want to charge the 69 cents to your credit card?"

I felt so accused of mismanaging the world's funds that I felt prompted to explain my transaction:

"It's a debit card, it works both ways!"

She took it as my apology for disturbing her peace.

The next day, after my bank errands to manage my money better, again, 24 hours later, I wished to sit down in the shade, just for a few minutes in a relative peace of a steady noise created by the traffic before I'd take a stroll back to my place.

In this part of town with independent stage theaters, everyone seemed to have an attitude, I was observing from my sidewalk café chair on the cross street, as if people competed at who was more obnoxious; the main street serving as a corso, a cat walk, a showcase for that purpose.

Suddenly a walking, smoking man in shorts and a pink polo shirt, clutching a book passed by. I examined his steps, and became almost positive this was the yester-nut, crossing my path again.

He was quiet, expressionless, and asked the girl sitting next to me if she minded him smoking. The girl closed her book, and left. The man grabbed her chair, moved it further away, and kept on smoking until his cigarette died. He dragged his chair back, and made himself comfortable at my table, as if he was sitting there before I had come, without saying a word.

I was curious about his book. Something must have happened in the past 24 hours. He wasn't any longer doing his mad mantra, and hitting himself over his forehead. Once he dropped the cigarette butt, I could read the title of his book: Tao Te Ching.

While he was twisting his heel on the cigarette butt, his cell-phone rang, playing a tune, but he wouldn't answer.

I kept on looking at my open notes when he asked me if the music bothered me. I said – no. I was just wondering in my thoughts about his ringing phone.

He said I was reminding him of Ruth without looking at me. I said I didn't know who Ruth was. Oh, she's from Six Feet Under, a TV character, a mother of a family who runs a funeral parlor. I thought – Oh, my goodness, thank you very much, and said out loud:

"I don't watch television."

"I don't either," said my nut, "but this is one show I never miss. Ruth is very beautiful."

What could I say to that? Thank you very much. I began packing slowly my things, and he noticed that.

"Am I bothering you?" he said.

I had to gently, but firmly answer the truth – no, I wanted to rest a little, and now I was ready to go again. I picked up my shopping bag. He asked quickly:

"Can I buy you something?"

I lifted my half-gone iced tea, and gave him a gentle smile. His face had no expressions. Maybe he had exhausted all of his energy yesterday on listening to his body that was telling him 'Stop thinking!' But today was a new day. He was on his Tao. And I was on mine.

I hope not to cross the paths again, because it would surely feel as though I've got a nutty suitor in my path, and that there was only one Tao.

8

SIT DOWN FOR A MINUTE

Mary would never believe she'd go to a dentist to relax. Coming as requested 30 minutes earlier to fill out the forms gave her an extra time to sit. Just to sit.

She was feeling like a marathon runner. When she was asked to follow a white coat to the booth, and sit in the dental recliner during her first visit, her analogy went further to the film of the same name in which Sir Lawrence Olivier, who sometimes competed with Orson Welles over a bigger success, tortured Dustin Hoffman's marathon man as the Nazi dentist by drilling his healthy front teeth in the raw.

When Mary declined any pain relieving injection, the student dentist said with worry and surprise in his voice:

"You're brave!"

How to explain that she wanted to feel what was happening, what was in the sync as her, herself, and no one else, even if the tooth discomfort should be the case?

Why? Being kicked around, moved about like a box, or like a piece of furniture might have reduced her sense of surroundings as a friendly environment. An analogy, if it wouldn't sound really crude and cruel, might be a natural disaster survival, including the necessity to carry along only a few most important belongings.

Working without pay, just for the 'staple food', and the dubious safety of a roof above her head, a shower once in a while, washing and drying her sparse clothes, super-expedient coloring of own hair – cheap and unseen – in a stained sink used for rinsing mops and paint brushes in the basement, all that reminded her of an old tale about a big flood, and a small frog who survived in it by 'stomping water' until the high waters subsided, and the ground came back under its feet.

The past before the big flood seemed so remote, and hard to believe with what back then looked like Mary's life, which might be happening by her own design. It was an illusion.

The only explanation she could think of was that she fell out of a favor of an ancient, capricious god who wasn't satisfied with the outcome of his creation. Marsyas challenged Apollo, and was terribly punished; but Apollo would have to be a pretty insecure god if he'd feel challenged by Mary's sonnets! One shouldn't forget about Midas, the judge of the famous musical contest, who was rewarded for his choice with ass' ears by irritated Apollo. Who was he? Midas was the Phrygian whom Dionysos empowered with the legendary, treacherous, golden touch.

Mary really felt as if her skin was peeled off live for some reason, that was why no numbing of her mouth at the dentist didn't seem too difficult to survive. This time as well. She signed her name at the receptionist desk, and sat down.

To a naked eye, to an outsider, Mary's past and her

present would be inexplicable: brushing shoulders with Hollywood mega-stars, being driven to the set with major British actors in the same car, occupying own trailer during a shoot, and now washing dishes, sweeping, serving food, sleeping barely five, six hours on a sofa, or other make shift bed in an indescribable space where recently a big grandfather's clock got wound up by the owner, and began ringing mightily, like the Big Ben every half hour all night long, right next to her head. To move her bed? Sorry, no vacancy...

Mary happened to be a part of this private, somewhat pretentious, busy establishment where she has been staying now for months to survive the time of the big flood by which the capricious gods must have blessed her with for a reason.

If Mary was to turn the pages in her life even further back, she'd see a similar pattern of the past periods of 'successes' and 'falls from the favor' as well: performing on stage, and suddenly washing hallways and steps in freezing cold apartment buildings after her years of engagement was abruptly terminated, because she needed income.

Later working with blind children, or with old and sick people which she regarded as a gift however, and always doing a lot of walking, by the way. One really old lady, she used to visit to help cleaning an impossible mess, bathe, and feed her, used to say:

"Just sit down for a minute."

There was hardly a place Mary could squeeze her small butt in. Piles of stuff cluttered the whole house: many years old, dusty, brownish newspaper, chimneys of books no one read, scattered bags of food bank groceries her son was weekly bringing in, ancient cans and bags in the cupboards. No one stayed there working for long, so unbearably heartbreaking.

Aside of Mary's exhausting work in exchange for 'room and board', her current, unpredictable, small income was expected in her bank account from stepping in for sick or otherwise absent teachers of three to five years old 'little friends'. Big emotions, big mysteries disclosed, tying of shoelaces learned; magical things were happening every day. Mary got to know almost all of the children.

There was a ducky boy with a tennis ball haircut who liked playing with girls, but couldn't handle his roughness, and they would run away making him angry. As soon as the snow ceased to lie on the ground, and the children began playing in the garden, he turned into an athlete:

"Watch my awesome dismount!" he'd say with a lisp, and struggle to climb as fast as he could manage onto a bar and performed his 'awesome dismount'.

There was a boy with Chinese features who was quite passionate about bus routes, time tables, schedules, rules and regulations, and fire alarms, maps for safety escapes, and such. He would draw a huge page full of numbers – 'route 4: Washtenaw to the Transit Center!' His announcement sounded like a friendly bus driver's voice, or rather a friendly recording. He took Mary on a detailed safety tour of the whole building.

There was a Korean boy who wouldn't wear gloves even during the coldest weather. Inside, he'd take his shoes and socks off with a silly smile, and wouldn't put them back on. So attached to his cot he was that it took lots of teacher's talking, and his screaming when attempting to make it disappear, and he always won – his little day bed meant his safety zone. His English was very partial; any time an Asian teacher, or a student showed up, he'd visibly cheer up; his stress dropped to a zero, and he'd crawl on the floor with cars, bubbling like a motor with his nose running as well, barefoot.

When he heard music, he'd jump up, and dance side to side like a pendulum with a blissful glee.

There were three girls who'd always plot something secret in the corner, and delegate willing boys to carry large blocks, pieces, or objects to build a house with. They argued a lot with bent arms resting on their waist, and crumbled faces with lips stretched downward.

There was a blond boy with a haircut like the Little Prince telling Mary long stories in rich vocabulary about monsters in his room at night. He was often building space ships carrying good guys to beat the bad aliens. The building took more time than the play, and the space ship usually ended up on the 'saving shelf', later forgotten.

There was a black Indian girl who always got away with no sleep in the afternoon, and managed getting a teacher to read to her.

There was a Russian boy who walked around with his arms apart like a sailor, mean expression on his face, acting out frustration from the second language struggle, and his inadequacies, sometimes crying for a long time for his mom after waking up, until Mary began dropping some Russian words here and there. He'd often call Mary close, and demanded her to stay with him, as if hiring her for playing with him alone. His violent and angry fits gradually decreased.

There was a boy of Moravian parents who wanted to blend in so much that he would insist on playing the games with the most notorious characters inspired by TV and video games. He'd use such a perfect American accent that if there wasn't for Mary, moved by his familiar clothing – the flannel checkered shirts and corduroy home shoes with buckles – it was hard to tell where his parents came from.

There was a tiny Chinese girl with a permanent

wonder in her face whose legs were stretching taller almost in front of Mary's eyes, who spoke with a raspy incantation of cartoon characters, and was always drawing pictures for the whole family: 'for my mom, my dad, and my big brother'.

There was a dark-haired boy, hugging his favored stuffed black and white cow in the sleep. He still needed a pacifier to fall asleep, but on his fourth birthday he made a resolution, and got rid of it. He loved playing in the tiny kitchen, dressed up in a long, sparkly dress, and a cowboy hat, asking Mary to button it up for him. She was welcome to come to the party when the food was ready.

There was a boy with a frozen awe, and a little disturbed question mark in his face who got once mugged by a huge teacher. He bit her in attempt to escape from being cornered. Stifled, Mary stood there, respecting the 'rules' of not to interfere with 'the more experienced teacher's methods'. After the horrible scene Mary offered him a drink of water, wondering how come the rest of the kids kept on playing, only once in a while glancing calmly, and with curiosity at the teacher whose inadequately covered frustration and anger perspired, and whose helpless voice continued repeating:

"Calm your body, calm your mind!"
Yoga? Regretfully not. The boy began to wear a necklace with a plastic tube hanging on it, a psychotherapist's prescription device for biting when he'd get agitated.

Some of the teachers have developed their educational methods for the three years old children, using 'techniques':

"Go and sit in that blue rocker by yourself for a while, you weren't friendly!" when a child was crying. Just like we used to be sent 'to the corner', Mary recalled. The child might be hungry, and even tired, brought in hastily without a breakfast in the morning, could she not? The teacher's righteous, and calmly satisfied face felt chilling to Mary while telling the inconsolably crying girl who must have already forgotten the reason for her tears:

"You still aren't being friendly!"

Mary couldn't interfere again, because of the 'rules', and not having witnessed the scene from the beginning. She just stood there helplessly, saddened.

There were blond boy twins with a little brother who'd follow them everywhere. The three acted as a bully squad not minding teachers' prompts. They must keep their German parents busy!

There were two sisters who loved reading and telling stories very creatively, especially the well known ones:

"And the princess... who was pretty and young... turned into an old hag... She ate that apple... and got poisoned...and died..." And thick noodles would pop out from her nose, making big blown bubbles while she'd produce a huge, satisfied smile. This was the younger one. The older one got everyone on their toes in the school's green room, and almost all children would follow her as wild animals, bunch of cats, or witches.

There was a boy from Latin America, adopted by a lesbian couple who was always using his 'outdoor voice' inside, performing movements and lines from the video games, speaking for all characters:

"Hurry, we must hurry! They are coming!" He'd glance at Mary if she was paying attention to his clever games. Restless, he'd go from one thing to another, compulsively abandoning the teacher's offered 'choices'. His computer heroes were his main focus. Mary was hoping to hear his addressing of the parents – two moms – or was one called dad? How did he feel about that? He would, like most of the children, wear his shoes backwards, the left shoe on the right foot, and vice versa.

One Hanukah boy would ask which shoe goes on which foot after he'd wake up, then he'd sit on his cot, and took a long time to fit the shoe on his foot, never checking with his eyes what were his hands doing, taking the shoe off repeatedly, and putting it back on, for it just never felt right in there. His 'elsewhere' expression told Mary how that elsewhere was important to him, soaking up all of his concentration; the shoes were perhaps supposed to get on by themselves. Gradually, he'd come back in the room, and his eyes would see Mary:

"Would you, please, help me?" he'd sigh like Sisyphus.

There was a three years old girl of Hispanic heritage whose grave facial expression made her seem much older; in fact her mother's face looked child-like compared to hers. Her language evolved quickly using long, elaborate sentences; she'd sit even on the floor like a lady reminding Mary her of doll when she was little. When the girl didn't like what someone did to her, she'd just quietly hit, or bite them with full strength and focus without getting upset. When a teacher rushed over to stop her, and console the crying, hurt child, she would simply raise her eyebrows in surprise with that sleepy, doll-like, pale face.

There was a chubby-cheeked little girl with a messy, long, brown hair who'd suck her thumb while falling asleep. She'd tickle with the other hand the arm of whomever was sitting by her.

There was another tiny German boy with a rounded smile, full of miniature teeth resembling a small sea creature, running in soft, toddler's shoes, happy to hear someone saying 'Auto' instead of 'car' and 'Zug' instead of 'train'.

Then there was a dark-haired boy with an angelic name, matching it with his appearance who once stood up in the middle of the lunch, and when Mary asked him to please sit down and finish eating, he'd say:

"I can't sit down, I have a poopy diaper."

"Would you like me to take you to the bathroom?"

"No, I'm not done pooping," he answered seriously and very concentrated while the rest of the little friends continued with their lunch equally seriously, enjoying their food.

Then there was an Asian girl with a strong bone structure and a distinctly square-shaped face who hardly ever said a word. She was ridden daily on a stroller to the school by a petit, wrinkly grandpa in a freshly ironed shirt who bowed in place of a verbal greeting. Mary believed – since he bowed like that every time she saw him – he was doing it to express his humble gratitude for his granddaughter's opportunity to be schooled. It was Mary's assumption dating from the times she used to read the Fairytales from the Land of the Dragon; an educated man was the most appreciated, and always at the top of the whole society.

Time had passed while Mary was entertaining herself picturing all the kids she could recall, perhaps to create a composite sketch for her crying heart.

The waiting room was filled now with less breathable, recycled air by many patients. A woman in a hospital uniform began calling one by one inside, loudly describing what will be done to them, almost with a sadistic gusto. Mary's name wasn't called.

She checked the time – goodness, two hours have passed! At the receptionist desk, a woman explained to Mary patiently that was the way it worked, sit down for a minute. How could have Mary disappeared from their list? Hasn't she signed her name two hours ago? The receptionist searched the records, and could not find her…

Gone, Mary was gone. She has vanished in two hours! Where has she gone? Could one plain disappear by thinking about what one's heart was missing? Maybe so, gone to find it.

The receptionist's seat was empty. Disappeared for her lunchbreak. The other one on duty found Mary's name to her surprise right away, and said – just sit down for a minute, we'll get you in as soon as possible, you've been put on the waiting list.

In the hall, with the typical old plastic stench, mixed with the decades lasting lack of fresh air, the blank faces of the remaining dental patients waiting on the washable chairs shifted Mary's focus to their staring at the television screen. She could only read in their faces what they were watching, being seated by the wall on which the television was mounted. Mary hasn't watched television for many months, maybe years, only occasionally.

The voice of the anchor sounded so disturbingly by soap, and out of place when Mary finally heard what she was announcing. The same news on the radio was bringing the reports from the recent terrible 7.9 Richter scale earthquake in the Sichuan Province in China with much more authenticity. Through the time Mary was waiting, the news were being updated, and they must have gotten to her whether she listened, or not. Mary's heart went there along with her thoughts about the little friends, and simultaneously about the people Mary missed. What was her marathon compare to the earthquake in the Sichuan Province? But what if what was happening to one, was happening to all, and vice versa? One extremely visible, the other absolutely invisible?!

How come? However fantastic and incredible this unequal

comparison appeared to be, Mary intuitively believed there was a link. Someone was running along. Someone who wanted to win that race over her. And that someone was mistaken in their assumption Mary was interested in running at all. In fact, Mary found herself rather being run, chased, and haunted. But since she has found herself in the midst of a race, it would be perhaps – and hopefully – a longer trip to go back, even if she knew which way to turn, and retrieve her steps to the beginning, to the start, and made sure she'd never get on that road if it was in her power, indeed.

Was there anything at all in the past Mary could identify as the first step on this exhaustive, and vain path which was far from her own chosen path? It seemed more like Mary was led there. Who'd wish so many struggles for someone else?

Coming back to the idea that Mary fell out of a favor of an ancient, capricious god who wasn't satisfied with the outcome of his creation didn't help. Mary didn't believe in ancient, capricious gods. What she believed in was love with which was this world created. Only people are capricious and clever with ill wishes for others, and fortunately – they are in minority.

Of course, things were more complicated. Why was this little girl deadly allergic to peanuts, for example? Why do earthquakes happen in the populated areas, and not only where nobody lives, and why on certain dates?

A hesitant, young, soon-to-be dentist staring into a folder attracted Mary's attention. Perhaps the pronunciation of Mary's name stalled her smooth entrance. Mary got up with hope her waiting was at the end.

"Hi, are you trying to call my name?"
The white medical coat turned toward Mary and said with relief:

"How do you pronounce your full name?"

Mary told her, and she radiated a smile:

"With a Z?"

"With two of them."

"How beautiful!"

Then she reiterated Mary's tooth story quite accurately.

"We'll try a permanent amalgam; however this is not the usual way – but we'll do it, since you've lost your temporary filling so quickly."

They went through the same conversation about Mary's refusal of the pain killers, almost to the word.

"You're brave," she said just like her predecessor.

She worked quickly with a firm touch, and the thought Mary might be experiencing discomfort didn't seem to cross her mind.

At the register, she presented Mary with an imprint of the treatments and their cost. Mary didn't object. After all, this was hopefully her last visit for she insisted on the permanent filling.

Mary paid the balance of a hundred dollars. A little money will be still left in her account, and she'll walk back quite rested. No need for any bus money! The whole afternoon of peaceful meditation close to a spa treatment cost only a hundred bucks. And all they seemed to ask of Mary was to sit down just for a minute.

The student dentist's hand's gentle touch drilled a bigger hole in Mary's tooth almost painlessly, and cemented it up fast with amalgam. Mary's tongue kept on testing the novelty in her mouth on the way to the establishment, where the grandfather's clock rang every half hour; but until late night she wasn't going to be reminded of its Big Ben... or Big Bang?

Something felt strange on that familiar street Mary walked on to care for the 'little friends' every once in a while.

As if in the mean time, a shift of some sort has occurred in the outside world while Mary dwelled mostly inside herself. A Parallel Universe perhaps?

She began to test the street with her eyes as thoroughly as her tongue felt the cemented hole inside her mouth. On the corner yard of the cross street, a small truck was being loaded with a chain saw. Next to it there has grown a huge wooden object: maybe a giant tooth? The woodcutter was rushing as if he didn't want to be caught at a crime scene.

Mary kept on staring at this raw piece of wood, passing by on the other side of the street. Instead of a giant tooth from the front view, she was looking at a sky reaching, enormous hand. It must have been speedily chopped out of a huge piece of wood while she had endured her dentist visit.

If she tilted her head, the sculpture seen from yet another angle resembled a drawing of her own hand she had made recently as a birthday wish for someone special. She mailed it a few days before the catastrophic earthquake, in fact.

Why does this feel like ridiculing her gesture? Ancient jealous gods sending chain saw artists?

Well, said Mary to herself, let's see if we can sit down, and write a new love sonnet between the top of an hour and its next half, squeeze ourselves quietly between the grandfather's clock's Big Ben's strikes, shall we?

9

HOOVER

He was given his first name after one of the Presidents' last name, but we'll call him Hoover. He represented the Wonder of Vanishing, as if it was the reason for his being.

He wasn't even three years old when his smiling mother, and his laughing father, both hard working, entrusted his existence for eight hours a day to a well chosen institution with chairs and tables, toys and games, indoors and outdoors, all for his size, the diminished world designed with the best intentions by grownups for children of his, and similar age.

Yet Hoover was suspicious that a very little thought was given to his real needs. Fortunately, his gift of being an outspoken orator often rescued him:

"That's NOT how we do it!!!" he'd use his voice potential to the top when an otherwise patient lady whom he was supposed to call by her first name – but who can remember them all – handed him a piece of toilet paper assisting him in the

bathroom. She seemed really startled when explained this:
"That's NOT how we do it!!!"
Instead of disposing off the paper in the trash, she made that terrible mistake, and dropped it - unused - into the toilet.

Hoover got really disappointed. Now what? All his work was spoiled: he managed to stand still, while the lady was removing his - dry - diaper after his nap; he aimed successfully into the toilet of which he lifted the seat himself, and helped the pee to come out without one drop missing the toilet bowl. Even holding up his long red shirt he remembered! And she makes that horrible move, and tears off a piece of a toilet paper:
"That's NOT how we do it!!!"
Whatever she was saying about people doing things differently in the bathroom just like in life with a surprised tone of her voice, as though this was a major revelation for her, reckoned pointless. She just spoiled his work.

Then she continued on with an unspeakable mistake of dropping the tissue into the toilet bowl which – what else he could do than fish for it with his bare hand? – she, seeing this rescue and remedy of his work – flushed! Not even asking, considering the fact she was supposed to assist, and not spoil what he had so successfully accomplished. She flushed the toilet! She was supposed to wait for him to shuffle to the flush handle with his pants still down, and answer his important question, as always:
"Up or down?"
First time she heard the question, she stared at him like a dummy, not hearing, or understanding such a simple thing! Then she finally answered:
"Down."
With a relieved smile, resembling his mother, he pushed the

handle down, and quickly covered his little ears, for the noise was expected to pierce them. He always waited, until the swirl of water disappeared in the tube, in the bottom opening, taking everything else along.

What if he pulled the handle up? What would happen then? Maybe the swirl would explode upward, and shoot him up in the sky without anyone else? Even without the lady who dropped the toilet paper in the cocktail down there?

Would he ever land back on the ground without wings, or remained forever in the space? Never saw this lady whose face would look up in astonishment, as he was disappearing among the clouds like a spaceship? Never saw his smiling mother who never hinted any of this business, or his laughing father who after eight hours of work would come to get him outside in the playground:

"That's NOT how we do it!!!"

Hoover screamed as loud as his voice stretched, and squished the lady's arms furiously, losing his gift of words at the moment, because the sequence of events was more rapid than his repetition of the words which he was hoping to stop the unfortunate derailing of his order with. The words, the tool grownups use to agree or not, were useless in this case.

Was it perhaps the mystery of the bathroom, the swirls of this 'not-at-home' place which could divert, or flush down the natural course of things?

He threw his pants at her in despair, his gift of words turned into a torrent of tears, howl of screams and swords of waving arms.

"Are you trying to make rain?" said the lady gently. Hoover's small ears alerted his big heart.

"What?!!!... No," he replied, "those are my... tears," and he touched one to make sure.

"Oh," said the lady satisfied with his answer.

"Are you trying to make wind?" she asked another unusual question.

"What?" asked Hoover again with more interest, because he too could feel the air moving around as if the wind was picking up.

"I thought you were trying to make the rain fall," the lady pointed to one of his tears that stopped in its motion from falling down his cheek, perhaps also surprised, asking – what?!

Hoover shook his head. His arms calmed down, as the lady's words reached little Hoover's big heart, and her pain went away as well. She could slowly wrap around his tiny bottom a clean diaper saying:

"Your squeeze really hurt, Hoover... Could we, please, give each other a hug, and be friends again?"

He looked at her solemnly; his deep eyes moved sideways to study each of hers, left to right, and his compassion opened his tiny arms. He embraced the patient lady.

Perhaps she was also confused by the swirls of this 'not-at-home' bathroom, and felt his pain which he was giving her back by waving mightily his arms making wind. She hugged him back, and helped him into his pants; Hoover could finally leave the bathroom.

When the children are let outside, it means someone is soon coming to take them home. One can never be sure of it, and as one by one vanishes with their grownups, the anxious waiting turns the little friends into dangerous drivers, sloppy climbers, goofy sliders, fierce attackers, or unwilling players.

When one of the many doors around the building opened, and Hoover's laughing father ran out to the playground to catch up with his offspring's energetic course, Hoover's tense face lit up.

His laughing father grabbed on his arms, lifted him in the air with much joy, and began swirling and spinning Hoover who was flying high in the air, orbiting like a satellite around his father, thrilled by the flowing current, the smudged rotating shapes, his light, dizzy head in the breeze created by his flight, firmly held by his father – whose knowledge of Hoover's daily wrestling with the world of strange forces designed by grownups, was limited.

10

THE TATTOO COUPLE

The first time seen, they appeared to be friendly neighbors from the same building getting on the bus at the Manor stop, named by the apartment building complex visible from the bus.

Its name was a misleading euphemism, if suggesting one of those pseudo Greek palaces with a row of white columns in the front. This concrete structure held as many apartments as possible, designed with a cookie cutter to serve as an affordable housing complex for people in need, assuming from so many passengers in wheelchairs, war veterans in their distinct caps, or clients who needed social services for various reasons. Their aides also traveled often from that same stop.

The face of the building was sliced up by railings on each floor into squares with entrances, and all balcony doors presumably led to a small apartment. Each square spoke of intentions of the inhabitants to enjoy life under the circumstances.

Almost every balcony was equipped by a couple of plastic white chairs, or even an outdoor, weather permissible grill, a bicycle here and there, brooms, and buckets, and undistinguishable rubbish which cluttered the space inside the apartment a long time ago. Not many flowers adorned the balconies, although it was yet late summer.

When the two traveled at the same time, the smaller of the two usually sat by the window, and the large one by the aisle side. At first they seemed both men; the small one with an imprinted permanent child like smile, and shiny eyes with long eyelashes, straw color, thinning, fuzzy hair; low cut arms on his undershirt were exposing bright tattoos, covering almost his whole torso.

The large person usually wore one of those baggy unisex sweat suits, not revealing much of anything. The smaller was often leaning closer during their conversation to hear all that was said, and his cheerful reactions offered an explanation that these two were a happy couple.

One day, the large one traveled in the opposite direction alone. It became clear it was a woman from the way she treated the things in her purse.

Next time they again sat next to each other on the bus, the small man by the window, they whispered to one another and giggled, the woman placed lightly her large hand on the small man's bare thigh with quite an intimate gesture. He seemed to shiver with delight. After everyone got off the bus at the transit center, they exchanged words upon which the small man pulled out a wallet from his back pocket, and searched in. He handed to the large woman a twenty dollar bill. She looked pleasantly content, and gave the man a child like smooch on his gathered lips. She needed to bend down for that kiss, and then she hid the money in her pocket. They parted.

The small man's saddened eyes found a young blond woman walking by. He began to follow her, light-footed, alone on the sidewalk, and couldn't take his eyes off of her. She cared nothing about his amorous pursuit and a little foolish, unconcealed perusing of her.

Another time the large woman traveled by herself from afar, perhaps where her job was. She reached inside her purse for a small book that could have been printed for one of those special occasions with a theme. Upon a glance, it was a book of sonnets, perhaps found in a second hand store to where it was brought by someone who no longer wished to keep it.

The list included glorious poets, like Shakespeare. In the murky, a little morbid bus light reading of the verses posed a strain on the woman's eyes; nevertheless she leafed through a few sonnets, and lingered on one or two with a dreamy expression, touched, and connected to her own romance. She closed the book quite early, before her stop came, and just sat there with her thoughts taking her someplace.

It wasn't obvious the two lived in the Manor, but quite probable. One could try to guess which balcony belonged to their place, and how that place might look inside. Who was in charge of which part of their household, who did which chores, and what was their way of entertaining: if they watched television side by side like everyone else at the prime hour, or stared into each other's eyes in rapture, holding hands.

What brought them together, how did they meet? Were they after all really just friendly neighbors in the same building at first, or have they perhaps met in a tattoo parlor, since the large woman was also decorated with a few colorful tattoos on her hand and lower neck. It could be only seen when it was warm enough for her to wear lighter, sleeveless clothing.

Or was the little man on some fixed disability income, and the large woman his nurse, or aide, at least at the beginning, and their mutual fondness had developed gradually from that care?

It would be difficult to imagine the small man in charge of caring for the large woman, although not impossible. There are large, patient mammals, aren't they, who adore their miniature friends, and are very protective, and fond of them. They don't read sonnets, however.

One sunny day, the small man was seen rushing madly on a busy street in down town. His eyes focused on some important idea, his mouth vocalizing it, his lips seemed repeating it over and over with an excited expression; maybe he didn't want to be sidetracked by any young, blond woman this time, that was how important his mission must have been; his picturesque arms bent in the front, his small legs in shorts beating the concrete sidewalk with his idiosyncratic light-footed pace.

One block below in the park, the large woman was seated on a bench like a statue cast in bronze, in harmony with the architectural design, motionless, and thoughtful. One could question if they knew about each other, behaving so differently in such a shrunk span of time and space?

They both made it on time to the next scheduled bus from the transit center. The small man still catching breath, his tattoos shiny with sweat; the large woman's illustrated hand fondly rested on his thigh.

When the bus took off shortly, the small man's breath calmed down, and the large woman's head tilted toward his; he lifted a plastic bag from between his bare legs, and pulled out a vinyl record. It was one of those old Motown records with the typical, brownish photos.

They both were pointing their fingers at the song titles, and at the faces on the pictures, naming everyone with delight in their eyes. The large woman began to hum quietly one of the songs.

One could picture how they spend the time together now: with their precious record collection and an old record player, singing, and maybe dancing too, cheek to cheek.

11

THE HATE MACHINE

He listened attentively not only because the theme was so captivating, but her tone of voice has always inspired his musical ideas. They kept coming from underneath the layers of words, activities, sounds that accompanied them all.

She knew him deeply without thinking about his behavior which could to a stranger, or a less sensitive and generous person seem distractive, and even be considered as self centered, because in the middle of the most interesting and climactic part of the story his eyes would stop moving as if not following what was being said.

His eyes would become more luminous with that soft glow of the light blue sky color. But she knew very well he was with her completely, and sometimes she paused not to get back his attention, but to enjoy his dreamy expression. She knew a new song was being conceived while she was passionately sharing what were her prep times for writing. This process of loving exchange has only remarkably refined over those many years they have known each other.

She couldn't enjoy more the whiles than when she overheard his early morning musical composing sessions, especially when he worked on something for own pleasure, and wasn't pressed for time, impatiently and deliberately erasing what he'd call 'rubbish'.

She wouldn't dare to comment on his work, even when he occasionally asked for her opinion; she just adored his ways he expressed sometimes sad, doubtful, troublesome thoughts of his so very brave, loving, all-considering heart.

This time she paused for a different reason than soaking in his inspiration. This time her own thoughts dashed rapidly, propelled by her emotions of determination to capture them in a very unique story – like most she ever told, or wrote – and he was one of the very few who could tell how much of its material was not fictional.

"So you were saying this is about children?"

"Yes. And mothers. There is a very old Serbian dirty saying; as you know, some nations belittle the intelligence of another countryman, and some use the coarse language in relation to parents, out of which the worst is to slander mothers."

She was so wrapped in her thoughts that her sluggish putting away the clean dishes came to an almost complete stop.

"Right. I can't stand it."

He took the plates, and then a beer jug from her hands.

"Me neither. But some of them bring out messages from afar. The one on my tongue is this: 'Ciacia te za karto!' Your dad paid with you his card debts. It's the dirtiest saying there is, I was told... by my mom once."

The old glass beer jug seemed to remind her of the childhood.

"Sounds really ancient."

He carefully set the jug down. A flash back sifted itself through, relating the old beer jug to a place he'd bought it as a present for his parents, a memorable item of long ago past times. Now it served often as a vase for flowers.

"I mean, using it as an image for some modern practices. I read how in the medieval Spain the *comprachicos* stole children, and held them for years in body disfiguring chairs to sell them for entertainment."

She picked up on the chore she was doing, and at the same time kept her theme while noticing his gentle taking over, and then again yielding when she had caught up through their eye contact.

She was really fond of his generosity manifested in such a simple manner, like using daily his collection of old dishes, glassware, cups, and precious art objects. He knew she touched everything with an amicable respect. Those things possessed qualities meaningful perhaps only to him.

She was moved every time by the scale of his emotions. No idolatry of objects, attachments to things of value, or the price tag. Sheer beauty, and memories; every object meant a life story. The jug she now held was released from her clasp, and placed on the spacious cupboards. She paused to allow his comment:

"We used to watch from our windows the kids in the neighborhood going across the street with a jug like this to get tap beer on Sundays around the lunch time."

"Pork roast, dumplings, and cabbage?"

He laughed.

"It's amazing we grew up in the same part of town…"

He nodded:

"Christened by the same river."

"After lunch on Sundays, did you listen to the fairytales on the radio?"

"Sometimes."

"I did. At my mom's house."

"That was before we met, right?"

She only smiled in response, and diverted her thoughts back to the theme encompassing the conversation which was taking a sweet and distracting turn.

"There are kids today subjected to altering their minds from their given, and natural talents; for years denied to express their souls, and cleverly manipulated into 'useful', machine like objects; children are so impressionable, you see!"

"*Compra-* what? It sounds like a Gothic novel mixed with science fiction."

"Well – it can be looked at like that."

Her thoughtful pause suggested she might be sorting stuff out from a non-fictional point of view.

Children were always the theme that interested her. She considered childhood a difficult part of life for the dependency on adults who often didn't really understand what children needed for their souls.

"A while ago, in the school I sometimes help, a girl was terribly sobbing, held by a compassionate teacher who tried, but couldn't console her. I had the opportunity to find out what was the matter: her mother had promised to come in for the Valentine's Day's lunch like the other kids' moms, but she got so busy that she just didn't make it. That was a reason for crying... The girl cried also the next day at the same time... She was reminded of the broken promise by seeing the same image the next day: parents accompanying the kids in the classroom, and she – nothing! So she sobbed: 'Mamaaa... mamaaa!'"

"I was just like that," he inserted. "My mom used to play

classical pieces on the piano to stop my crying."

"Did it help?"

He just smiled, and outstretched his arm to gently touch hers.

"I remember my mom closing herself in the room, and playing passionately Chopin to dissolve her fury... Your mom knew you'd be a musician, and that music would always save you if nothing else was going to work out."

He didn't say anything again, and she could tell he was still missing his mother, regardless the time that had passed since she was gone. Then he re-iterated a well known fact bringing out a nostalgic smile on her face:

"I went to the college and got my degree to make my parents happier about doing music."

"Our graduation from the European schools wasn't very helpful here, was it...?"

"Our French especially didn't help us here, did it?"

She shook her head smiling. She was reminiscing on their correspondence across the Ocean. It was the sixties before the Iron Curtain fell; their parents were still young, younger than them now, of course.

"You know, I want to write this story to honor our mothers – there's never enough said about this."

"And..." paused he, searching for best words, "is there going to be also some of the personal account of... other loving?"

"I think it's inevitable," laughed she. "I was thinking about the disturbed girl," tried she getting back to the beginning of her trail, "and the striking way she cried so much for days. It occurred to me that there must be an underlined, deep reason that explains this disproportional, endless flow of tears. As if her mom was prevented from coming for the little girl to build mistrust, to plant a schism, a divide between the two females instead of bonding. Wait, I know you might say this is my

construction, my speculation. I am just sharing somewhat stranded ideas on this theme with you. I can't accept as the explanation that her mom got too busy to come, but won't bore you with the school schedule to prove my reasons."
She spoke rapidly, still echoing the little girl's distress.
"I believe there is a mechanism in place, invisible, but very real, which can set affairs in a desired motion with a precision of minutes, hours, days, and in the long run – years."
"You got my full attention!"
"Let's go for a walk, it helps my thinking, what do you say?"
"Oh, my old bones...."
Yet he got up, wrapped his long arm around her shoulders, and whispered to her ear:
"But I'll gladly stretch them."
"So will I. I really appreciate your sacrifice."
He laughed voicelessly at her statement, knowing she meant it.

The grassy riverbank still bore signs of winter. The soil was heavily breathing after the thick, white comforter of snow has melted.

He loved leading the way to places meaningful to him and reflect quietly on his own intimacies, and share this way the emotions hard to express in words. He's been like this ever since they met as children of twelve and fourteen, she thought.

She was speaking, and her almost tactile way of emotional connection to him kept on registering his state of mind. It was a continuous source of deep pleasure, and satisfaction for both. They were both rather visceral people, and shy in verbal expressions of praise that might in English sound cheap, like cheesy advertising.

Fortunately, their native language they shared allowed for a wide range of diminutives, and a unique, distinct, generational slang. The full and vast realm of familiar expressions, blissfully relieving misunderstandings, was found useful in their communicating which they cherished with joy in a somewhat minimalist way. It became their secret language on occasions.

She made him often laugh without trying, by the way she used words, and he learned not to correct her English too fast, because she didn't like the 'male', short efficiency of the colloquial talk, perhaps partly due her stubbornness in insisting on 'thinking for oneself', and thus using original thoughts in a less common language.

Colloquial speaking reminded her of the didactic Ecclesiastics. She liked Ecclesiastics in the past times of hardship, she found it comforting. The Book of the Proverbs as well. 'Vanity, nothing, but vanity' in English though seemed to shift the meaning of the saying toward 'the surface appearances being transitory'. In her mother tongue the translation felt as capturing more the mystical, and much more internalized experiences after tasting the life fully, and still not finding fulfillment. Later she appreciated the complexity of any language more, and enjoyed their charms including old sayings, and song lyrics, aiding her to feel more at home.

He has gone through the same path in learning English, but twenty years earlier, using goofy cartoons among other tools. He could relate to all of her struggle well, and that was why he treated her English weaknesses with chivalry. She certainly appreciated it.

His quick thinking, and a self-ridiculing sense of humor posed a challenge for her. She respected him with an overwhelming wonder, with her knees betraying her balance, and tears leaping unexpectedly to her embarrassment (after all these years!) – yet, she was far from being sentimental. And he was always, again and again taken by her incredibly modest material needs.

On their outings, he would bring her each time some place she hasn't been yet. This area was quite new to her, but familiar to him who had lived there for some years.

It was as if he demanded of her fresh eyes and awareness at all times, and wished her to keep own train of thoughts and activities. All very subtle, but quite intense, and involving all attention.

Sometimes she felt really exhausted after such a date, having come to that conclusion *post factum*. She thought her soul had grown wiser in many layers every single time. She was very grateful for all the challenges, more than willing to undergo them with a certain spongy thirst.

He's been always chivalrous and a natural leader, responding more to the audible and between the lines than to an argument and logic which he exercised in his amazing professional conversations with people in business. And still, when he was mistaken, he gladly admitted to it. He seemed always ahead of the game, sharp, sporadic, and careful in judgments, until the blanks got filled. Then he was satisfied.

This path along the swollen river yielded a free supply of thoughts, because it simply followed the straight direction, and was wide enough for both to stroll side by side. Occasionally, their arms would touch to realize their steps differed in length, and distracted their attention, until he reached for her arm, and adjusted his long steps to her shorter ones. Then she'd elongate hers. She was used to meeting things at least in middle, if not through.

She quietly adored the way he lifted her arm by the elbow, and inserted his arm resolutely in the opening; with his next step, she would feel their synchrony in walking as well as in the mood, and mutual thankfulness for being together.

To this day, she didn't care if it was pouring rain, scorching sun, or blowing wind, as long as they could feel each other like this. She would never take his presence for granted, and trusted blindly her faith in what she called 'a mirror effect', or 'as above – as below' of Hermes Trismegistus, the sensation of instant harmony, and mutual receptivity.

Her astonishment from that fact dated decades ago. With a faint feeling of internal blush she'd recall how naively she used to speak years ago, inflamed by the deep joy from his presence; he'd often refer to their past conversations, remembering them almost to the word, and claiming her statements to be inspirational, and wise; one time saying he used to feel she was like an older sister because of her insights. His enormous tolerance and generosity, expressed in subtle ways repeatedly astonished her, and moved her.

Again, with an internal shy smile, her giving-in knees reminded her why she revered this man so much. Certainly not only for his musical talents which elevated him to the highly respected, well deserved, and also envied position of fame.

The older they were getting, the more precious these walks became. All by themselves, no pressure, no phone ringing, just a chunk of private time. She really appreciated his willingness to listen. She had to learn how to relax before she expressed lightly her wish to go for a walk, just because his time was so dear.

He suspected her anxiety around his busy schedule which he successfully managed to follow with a wave of his arm in the midday saying – well, this can wait, I can only do so much, there is Life. And he'd peek at her load of work which usually also 'could wait.' This way her asking was pre-emptively rid of that uncomfortable pressure.

"Life is so short," escaped her.

He simply removed his arm from the loose holding, and wrapped it around her shoulder to better hear her dim voice which was about to carry out something from the depths.

"And we don't get to talk about everything that matters, cutting through the small talk and shallow pleasantries, straight to the heart. And then the time comes we don't dare to open that can of worms, and it's late, we'll never hear about our parents' childhood grieves, loves, dreams, memories of fears, pain, pleasant, and equally unpleasant surprises. Maybe that's why grandchildren can form a closer relationship with their grandparents, their communication is emotionally more tangible... Did you have a chance to talk with your parents about their lives as an adult a lot? And how did they see *you* as an adult?"

"Do you miss your father?" asked he instead.

"I guess, you can read better than I, what's underneath my words."

He smiled with a grave shake of his beautiful head. She could still see the teenage boy, and the young man, the man who called himself 'over the hill' before his fortieth birthday, and 'grandpa' not being yet fifty, and childless; she could see through the transparent layers his vibrating soul. Just as always, they were on the same wave length, often even when they had been far apart.

"I was spending much more time with my aged parents than when I was a kid... you know, don't you. When my dad got so ill, and mom needed help, then it all came together. I used to read to my dad from your manuscripts... when he could no longer see..."

She took a long breath which he noticed first with his acutely hearing ears. They continued walking for a few minutes in silence. He wished to listen to all of her thoughts happening inside, but his respect kept him from asking impertinent questions. Instead, he watched her expressive face from close. Better than words.

Her refined face, now with fans of shallow wrinkles, seemed deeply moved by the remembrance of his ill father she liked so much as a girl. Her unwilling absence during the hardest time for his family was made present by his reading of her first manuscript, and it was a powerful fact, an act of love.

"I used to miss my father when I was ten. Then I needed to learn to be on my own – as you know. I also missed my mom, but I never talked about it," she finally continued.

"You don't have to go on. I remember our conversations about it. You've always seemed very independent, dear."

"Well, I don't want to avoid the answer, since you gave me the opportunity to think out loud. There is a lot of mystery in my father's life. I don't believe he would have answered truthfully any of my questions when he got older. I would care not if he was buried with his shadow, the dark stuff that I wish I could express better, oozing like smoke, forming that shadow, and soiling everything, it seems. Like those ocean octopuses that spit ink to vanish in it." She paused.

"His adulthood I could possibly reconstruct with the help of my younger sister…"

"The one we bathed together..?" inserted he.

"Yes, you were about eighteen. She's now a mother of two, and drives a sports Mercedes… Does it feel a long time ago?"

His eyebrows changed positions a few times, hearing her youngest sister's brief, updated CV.

"Yes… and no, because you are with me now."

"Is that a good thing?"

"The first, or the second part?" he laughed so gaily from the pleasure to shift the conversation into this silly questioning which he always did just to see her eyes expressing the mirroring emotion.

She suddenly thought of Marilyn Monroe's statement in her charming autobiography, describing erotica as a continuum during the simple daily activities, like handing a cup of coffee to a partner.

"Both, no? The first would be sad without the second."

She didn't disappoint his expectations. She could feel she has exceeded them by already dropping everything she'd talked about, and by stopping the stroll. Was it that watery Moon sign of his making him so thirsty for affection?

"Because one would also feel old?"

She nodded.

"Do you *feel* old?" she asked.

His head swung to one side from the desire to shed light onto a different subject, away from the theme focusing too much on him.

"There's much of you who's wisely young!" and she threw her arms around him, grinning, forgetting her own age.

"Best compliment in many years... Imagine the other way around!"

"Sure, there's majority of those... old fools. Is that what you meant?"

He nodded and shook his head as well, and made a faint, unfinished gesture pointing at himself.

Their eyes followed two huge birds flying across the river gliding in a large oval through the air, and returning closer to the surface, until they smoothly landed with tracks of water in their wake.

"Herons, or storks? It would be early for the storks, wouldn't it?"

"Storks aren't common here."

He looked at her from below, like every time he got surprised.

"Hm…" smiled she.

"Can you tell the note they call?"

"I don't think I have the perfect pitch. When I hear a sound that is musical I try sometimes to guess."

"I bet you are good at determining a note. Can you tell this one?"

"It got higher… half a tone?"

He laughed voicelessly, and gave her a beautiful, humble, and short speech about his noticing noises, sounds which she could always hear in his music.

She could tell almost about any song where it was conceived: the sounds of the traffic in the busy New York City, or on the hooting and clinking Continental metro, or by the gushing Atlantic beaches with huge, gliding sea gulls, and gusts of whistling wind. But the best was when she could hear the silence in his songs, often accompanied with the few simple lyrics. She understood also through her own working process – that was anywhere, any time, under any circumstances.

She admired his labors. It's one thing to scribble a few ideas in a notebook, but another thing to orchestrate everything necessary to hold a finished record in one's hands! She told him her thoughts.

He leaned forward as if he was ready for more, his hands shyly slid into his coat pockets. These little expressive gestures always reminded her of having seen him doing them for over five decades.

"It's just so delightful to have known you for so long! Lots of things can be appreciated just because…"

They both quietly made a few steps; her gift of keen observation suggested they might be thinking about the same question.

"Yes… Why then?"

He looked at her quickly a little more than surprised, but feeling so very safe by her side he said:

"…you've never told a lie," unaware he quoted own lyrics.

"For some years I had nothing, but your songs… and then they became a part of me when I had no device to listen to the music… You've always thought of me highly; that's what kept me alive… And before I had your songs… when divided by the Iron Curtain… you represented a very real Hope, a living Hope for me. I've always missed you."

He released a long breath, as though walking across an invisible bridge between the present, and the past.

"Yes. Why then?" he repeated the question in a quieter voice. She nodded gratefully. Yet, she could never approach a serious theme in a conversation directly.

"Remember that time we were so much looking forward to see each other after so long, and you had work in Europe, and I could come also? When I arrived, we realized there was a mistake made in a span of a *month*, so we only had a couple of days together? You didn't say anything, until it was time for you to leave, and my two days were preset, busy with unimportant events that could have waited! How shaken I was! I was shy to appear as if I was curious about your celebrity status schedule… I sensed something was working against… our interests."

He made a little ridiculing sound. She always admired his attitude in these matters. That was why she couldn't tolerate the envious, and derogatory remarks made about him in her presence by certain local wannabes. The memories of those scenes still sickened her, even after the years. These people had no idea what a luminous character it took. She frowned her brows, and mentioned that to him. He waved his hand.

"You know, we live charmingly simply, but I know who you are! You could live... perhaps you've contemplated at some point a life - in the Castle," she grinned. "Maybe you should still attempt it..."

The thought escaped her unpremeditated. Her opinion about the stature of his leadership might have needed more of her personal endorsement:

"I've always seen and cherished that loving essence of yours, that bright warm light you emit..."

She managed to express this exalted feeling with a brief, beaming smile yet so plainly that he didn't struggle to accept its weight. She would hardly ever say anything like this to him during a candle-lit dinner. Bad taste, she'd warn herself. But in the rain, these words spilled out easily with the wave of her instant heart opening.

"That's nice," he breathed out. "I've always had in mind a stewardship. Is that what you called the Castle?"
She nodded.

"Not Kafka," she added with a grin. "And not politics. Power is a big temptation. "
He smiled:

"Well, my ideas would be rather radical, and people don't vote for those. Only in desperation, maybe."

He gave her some of his ideas about government, and she agreed, including the assessment of unwillingness to vote for what the popular voice claimed as the human right – love. She paraphrased out loud James Baldwin's statement about love never being a popular movement, and the populus not wanting to be free.

"I think it's about time people take love very seriously!"

It might seem their conversation was disjoined and fragmented when they continued on about hypocrisy by which he was less disturbed than she. He was much better exercised in wrestling its symptoms due the much longer cultural exposure to it. He quoted someone's wise words:

"You have to be secret about what makes you particular in the outer world."

"Especially about what is sacred to you," she couldn't help saying and simultaneously hearing in her head his earlier lyrics which at the time made her very worried about their misunderstandings, originating from her lagging English.

He assured her that sometimes he would feel stranded for not speaking their mother tongue for extended periods of time, and not being able to go back for decades, his sense of daily life there was rather sketchy, until they reconnected by writing letters to each other.

"By the way, I fell sick when I came home from that trip, my mom had to take care of me," he remarked at the end, recalling his travels to their homeland.

"Wasn't it often the case? Change of the climate?"

"Yeah, from China to the jungle."

"See, I believe, these were *not* our mistakes. These were the works of a mad watch-maker who wanted to play a god."

"Hm… so that's why… Our fates have been extraordinary enough."

She was waving her hand in disagreement.

"All I am trying to say is we *could* have been subjected to something like it," he clarified.

They both looked at each other with farther questions in their eyes, and she was very grateful he was taking her seriously.

"I haven't been very good at keeping my appointment book

up-to-date, but I don't need writing down things that matter to me most," he said thoughtfully.

"That's what I believe about you. Just like I was taken by the sight of your bright yellow notebook which I had assumed contained your lyrics, and musical ideas. See, that's your appointment book! I'm the opposite: I have to write down everything, it's helpful for the past reference, too."

"You were showing me your engagement calendar in that Greek restaurant. I began doing the same thing... So," he changed his tone of voice, "the mad watch-maker."

And she started slowly about her years of observations: how her choices were always made if not impossible, at least very difficult, the main ingredients being timing and distances, and later money, or better, the extreme lack of it.

How in the process of deciding, and at the end of each situation he was her mentor or consultant *in absentia,* because he always wished her best. And also how it often felt as if... someone was looking over her shoulder, or was stalking her, everywhere. What was continuously upsetting to her was the notion of misusing such a concept: if someone could design mad clock works for destructive purposes, how could have the whole world prospered from the opposite?

He was listening attentively, walking on her left, closer to the water for her to enjoy the view, his head glanced every once in a while at the resting birds on the meandering river.

She noticed how the birds' gently bobbing heads corresponded with the rhythm of their steps, and wondered if that was why he often peeked at them. She also enjoyed glancing at him, the river, and the birds.

"It's dissolved now, isn't it," inserted he after one of these quick glances.

"The mad clock works?"

He nodded. She had to think about it.

In the silence, while waiting for her answer, he began inventing other ways of how to measure time – on their terms, and by their needs. A unique, special clock for which he needed a name yet based on its functioning.

"At times," she continued hesitantly, and with difficulties, "the machinery was hard to detect, I almost forgot about it, as though it went underground, or someone new took over, or somehow a more advanced approach was in development; and each time after the less noticeable sum of mishaps, grievances, missed opportunities, or losses, and so on, much harsher events would occur."

"Do you have an example?"

"I think if we put together our motions that happened separately when we tried to communicate, for instance, we would see a pattern."

They began a long, chronological list of their travels, including the years in which traveling was seldom possible for her, or not at all. Soon, he couldn't stop shaking his head, recalling own intentions, and how he often ended up discouraged, assuming she was too busy with her life to pay attention to him. He admitted it was rather something other people would suggest, he trusted his feelings, but couldn't find an opportunity to speak to her.

In these delicate matters they were very similar: addressing them directly didn't suit their poetic natures, and the head-on approach could crush, or obscure such a soulful matter. They both respected each other to the speechlessness, and the usual pressure for time as an effective leverage wasn't helpful, rendering often lyrics, not common words. If there was each time just a little more time, these two wouldn't have needed any words. Then, another obstacle was space, just like in quantum physics, she thought, all interdependent.

The evidence became accumulative during the decades, creating an obvious pattern, impossible for her not to notice, mainly because of the tremendous emotional pain and strain she'd experience.

When they managed to see each other, it always felt almost like a miracle, and such situations found them both astonished and enchanted. And always, their hearts sunk upon parting, not quite understanding why was life so elusive.

She mentioned her reading of Nadezhda Mandelshtam's memoirs, one of its most difficult passages to read, describing how she just stood there, while Osip Mandelshtam, her husband and poet, was being picked up by Cheka, by two men in leather coats; Nadezhda's intuition telling her she'd never see him again, and how she never stopped blaming herself for not trying to stop them: scream, attack them with bare hands!

Then, she spoke about how after each of their face to face - increasingly more stressful - more dangerous events followed, how she felt their communication became every time more complicated, more difficult, and for periods of time impossible. That was when she began to pay attention to *who* had the personal interest in their unhappiness – *cui bono*?

Her conclusions were disturbing and frightening; soon she realized there was no one she could tell any of this. No friend, no relative, no stranger. Who would believe in the existence of what she named the Hate Machine?

And how she was getting busier and busier with just surviving, unable to live in any place for more than a very few years, chased out frightened, jobless, worried about him with the disrupted communication, leaving things behind, carrying fewer and fewer belongings with her, *omnia mea mecum porto*, abandoning technology – internet communication for the frightening emails disappearances, and quitting using her cell and mobile phones. How limiting!

She got cut off from those few friends who treated her as an eccentric, slowly aging, former beauty, now unfortunate. She didn't care. All she wished for was the Hate Machine broke down, believing it was affecting everyone, except they couldn't see it. They could not know what she – and him too, she hoped – held as the truth.

She needed his help; she needed the help from anyone who could do anything about the destructive machinery. She needed to topple the heartless, remote, but organized, and ever-ready operators with ill taste of humor whose sole function was to cover up their destructive intents.

Her vivid gestures accompanied her lists of evidence. He watched her hand movements as if she were dancing for him. Her side vision registered his eyes, and she got flooded with his warmth, discovering his changed ways of communicating, how he's grown wiser, more generous – they no longer had the whole lifetime ahead. He was just right there!

"Who would wish to create and operate such a mechanism, for god's sakes?! Who would have the time?!" he exclaimed. She would hesitate, shake her body, and then her head.

"You know the answer... don't you?" insisted he.

"I am not sure. Let it be a story, instead of a simple answer... I have many more questions. You are a wonderful listener, and *your* questions are superb!"

"I won't pressure you, of course, but if this ate much more than two thirds of our lives, I need to find out."

"Well, my dearest! Think about people who passed through your life who lied to you, that will give you a lot of clue. Think of the beautiful lies with sparkly eyes. Think what made you believe in them: fear? Getting stranded? Loneliness? I don't wish you falling into that guilty, flagellant mood. Use an internal microscope in admiration of the insect's elaborate disguise."

He stopped walking, bent down to pick up a flat rock, and threw it like a Frisbee on the water surface. Both watched the frog-like hopping of the stone on the river surface.

"What is it about jealousy...?" he didn't finish his question – the theme being enormous. Knowing her well, he only needed to punch the headline.

Her high perceptivity immediately grasped all his complex emotions behind the question, the prevalent being the battle between a betrayed trust, and almost blind optimism, originating in his love philosophy. She'd answer such a question a lot more plainly, if someone else asked it.

"A really jealous person – in my opinion – is someone who doesn't know what love is."

He looked at her surprised and relieved, glad he had found the courage to ask.

"A loveless person thinks of love as of addiction, that it is something unhealthy which must be cured. They feel appointed as experts on curing something so uncontrollable, childish, time consuming, impractical and costly – for they could use whatever you are giving away...

"And so they doctor you by administering the harshest methods, just like in times of the loony houses of the 18th and 19th, perhaps even persisting into the 20th century in many cases, with padded, windowless confinements, with icy water poured over your poor body unexpectedly, and later by the famous electrical shocks and lobotomy, all scientific and very medical, you see... and by ridiculing you and the subject of your love... It could be books, music, your cat, friends, even your children – just about anything you tell them you love...

157

n'est-ce pas?" she grinned in response to his head shakes. He knew exactly what she meant.

"You seem to have been tried on most of the cures. Any results?" he examined her face, smiling.

She shook her head, and thought quietly about the damage on one's soul by such a treatment.

"They can drive you... nuts, you know? You get scared that anything you love is worth of destruction, because you can feel their emptiness which they want to fill; their powerlessness once they hint the mighty love is missing them... Tell me, please, this is very important, has anybody ever told you, or suggested I was posing a grave danger to you?"

He finished his step in a slow motion, and appeared retrieved inside, yet with open ears, remaining taciturn. She took his silence as a yes, but didn't insist upon hearing it.

He pointed to a low brush at the foot of a river rock.

"Here lies my sweet, faithful cat."

She realized this was their today's aim from the start. She got hold of his hand without a big stretch, and he was glad she did that.

"What color was she?"

"All white, a kind of precious breed. I won some trophies with her."

"Was she perhaps hard of hearing?"

He looked surprised.

"Yes, in fact, she was practically deaf. That ended up her life."

"It looks very similar here to where my cat is resting. Born under a blackberry bush, buried under one as well. On the West Coast."

"She didn't lie either."

"Animals don't lie, that's a fact. People do."

"Animals can be taught 'appearances', no?"
She followed easily his quick thinking this time.

"This is wonderful that you say so, I have seen all kinds of animals – even wild ones, not only pets – to be a part of the mad clock works."

He turned around with a baroque gesture 'after you, *Madame*', and pulled up the collar of his coat, making sure she was also bundled up, scanning her face, uncovered ears, neck, hands, then inspected her shoes, if her feet didn't get soaked.

She began her quite unusual list of squirrels staring into her face for a long time from just a foot away; squirrels coming through a chimney in her place, full of fleas, that moved under her bed; squirrels stretched flat dead with tire marks in her path as if carefully placed for her to see; squirrels found dead in a bed & breakfast bathroom and thrown out for food to raccoons; the squirrel's frozen remains – a grim sight – which she was asked to bury. Then she reminded him of her meatless diet, and he'd make an understanding, tongued out – bleh! – sound.

She listed birds of prey landing in the city garden, and looking at her through the window; red robins following her on her way to work hopping from one tree to another, while their voices sounded like an electronic recording; spiders suspended at night above her head and aiming their telescopes at her for hours in her sleep; huge nonflying cockroaches making a weird noise; two cats performing together little stories for her – suggesting certain humans; other accounts with dogs and cats, namely animal injuries coinciding with major family events.

She also listed humans who acquired animal qualities, for example going to wash their hands multiple times in five minutes, and thus resembling raccoons' hygienic habit.

He was quite entertained by her vivid presentations of the

creatures at first, asking her to repeat how the stiff squirrel watched her closely while she was sunbathing. They frequently stopped for her little performances. As was the list growing, he began shaking his head more, and listened more carefully. Lots of his own instances seemed strikingly complimentary.

"One time in the afternoon," she added to her list, "out of the blue, a strange guy walked by my building with a pet magpie sitting on his shoulder under his long, greasy hair; he was talking to it, and it listened – you know, a magpie... they steal anything shiny..."

"A metaphor meant perhaps for someone else, not you..."

"*Touché*," she appreciated his remark, explaining the next stage of her observations concerning an odd, and a disturbing feeling of being exposed to all this bizarre stuff happening in front of her eyes that was making no sense to *her*.

On the other hand, there were also times when she was meeting people as if by someone's design as if that someone was interested in sending her messages which only *she* could recognize. For instance, she'd keep running into characters from the books she was reading – either people with the same names, or their obvious attributes. As if someone wanted to let her know they watched everything she was doing. She would tell him how creepy she'd feel, because all of it was based on knowing her intimate things, inclinations, habits.

There was another period of time when she was bumping into 'lookalikes', including relatives, some 'long time no see', mostly in a ridiculing manner, including *him*, or rather *his caricatures,* as if someone was trying to degrade him in her eyes, and all that for many weeks repeatedly – everywhere: on the streets, in places she was going to look for employment, on the public transportation. So very disturbing, when she had no contact with him, and no way to know how he was doing!

Sometimes it all felt like an automaton with a remote control; but these people, whom she called 'extras', must have been hand-picked for the close resemblances to the real persons only she could recognize; so someone she knew *must have been* in charge of that one-day operation when they all were shoved in her way. And if one day, why not every day, since this has been going on for many years?!

In their home town, she would notice her old friends changing drastically their behavior during a conversation, or more accurately their personality, including idiosyncrasies and character. At first, she contributed that to her immigration, and a long absence there which experiences her friends, who never lived outside the country, were unable to relate to. It wasn't true about all however, and she couldn't figure out why. She withdrew herself from most, flabbergasted, hurt, and confused, weighing the drastic changes, somehow related to her.

"Did you ever find out?"

"I think so."

"Why did they become so different?"

"Those who have changed so dramatically, whom I could no longer call friends, all without exception, came to a close proximity, or even stayed for a period of time, for example working, with one particular… person."

"I see. Hm. I bet I know who that person was."

She nodded.

"I bet you do – keep it nameless for now…"

"And when I needed help to at least make a few bucks to eat, and pay the basic bills not to end up on the street, and someone offered me a small job or a temporary work, they all got somehow punished."

She paused again, because she arrived to the chilling facts of several people's tragedies, including losing their lives. She decided to skip this part at this time. Hopefully and inevitably, during their evening sessions they will cover all important facts.

It was beginning to drizzle.

"Why did you pause? You don't need to hold anything back."

This time, it was him who mentioned another powerful passage from Nadezhda Mandelshtam's memoirs: about the benefits of going for a walk in the fields to make sure no one else could be listening to Osip's and Nadezhda's conversations.

His knowledge about the threat of misuse of the advanced technology today put his remark into a new context.

She continued with her list of what else was a part of the mad clock works: eating certain foods seemed to influence events, she noticed while staying with her relatives, for example; words, activities, like going for a hike, and placing objects in a certain order appeared to be another ingredient. It did make very little sense to her at times.

"Quite maddening, isn't it...?" he uttered. "How are you going to work with this reality to make it a story? Life is just much more powerful than any imagination, fiction..."

To a rhetoric question there was no answer needed. She nodded pensively.

"There were times I got so scared of being watched, and listened to that I tried to do things in the dark and quiet, or with my eyes closed, even write! It wasn't comforting; the fear didn't go away... I tried to pretend it was all my imagination, because whom could I tell about my experience without being suggested to visit a psychiatrist? In fact, a friend of mine, who suffered a drastic death of her husband from a heart failure at home, recommended me to get the same drug from her doctor, saying I would no longer feel anything."

"Did you?"

"No. Of course not. My pretending that it was all my imagination worked until the next event the mad clock works presented me with. For instance the subtle, but very frightening behavior of my father which I tried to explain to myself by his booze abuse. I have to say though I saw him only occasionally in the last years of his life."

"Well – one needs to undergo a treatment, or all's lost."

"Right. What's there to say, if his wife was a drug abuse therapist? My guts were warning me. His seductive sense of humor reminded me of the manipulative handling I used to be subjected to as a child. Was it to withstand things that cultivate insecurity? But I'd sort that out much later."

"Like?"

"When he got angry with me, he would not talk to me for days, disregarding my begging for being told why. Lots of solitude which is emotionally very hard for a child."

"That is. And how did it play out with the jokes together?"

"Well, he was absolutely unreliable – for example in being on time. And he always distracted my frustration, shame, and fear from his tardiness by making really funny jokes."

"I can see why you can be still nervous when we are running late…"

"Hm. Cover up. I couldn't stand that. It was basically lying, one just didn't dare to label own father a liar… My latest belief is that he turned an alcoholic purposely, to be useless, as a revenge, to send mixed signals; he would cover up his condition perfectly, of course, that's very symptomatic. At the same time, he wouldn't resign from playing his - false - role of a … patriarch."

"And his wife wouldn't see it?" He shook his head. "Self destructiveness is like a black hole!"

"Exactly." She added painfully: "I think he was very jealous of you all his life."

She couldn't go any further, finding out how upset this reminiscing was making her. She didn't feel armed enough at the moment to expand on her latest statement.

"Were you feeling lucky when we met?" he asked with a light giddiness, and she heard in his voice his own memories. She was instantly in a different world.

"Oh, was I feeling lucky? Do you mean the first, the second, or the third time we met? I've never stopped feeling lucky ever since the first time," she whispered, and shook her head many times instead of a lengthy monologue.

"I am looking forward to hear more comments," she managed to compose herself. "Some of my situations placed on a time line with your events might shed more light onto the mad clock works mechanism."

"What was the most difficult: the fear?"

She took her time to answer this important question.

"Fear is very crippling. Is it possible to imagine fear from… losing it? Or fear of not being sure whether you hold your own destiny in your hands? If you can't see God's Hand? In the smallest things, or the substantial decisions?"

"I can imagine it easily, it's very scary, I know. What else?"

"I'd say faith, faith in people."

"What did you do?"

"All kinds of helpful crutches, but when I was reduced to living out of a suitcase, and with no income for months – a real pilgrim, I dwelled inside myself so much, until I found faith in there, and told myself, that's where all the faith begins."

"How did it happen that you ended up with your suitcase like that?"

"Well – I went to search for you."

He stopped walking, and threw his arms wide:

"And you didn't find me…"

She nodded sadly. He sighed deeply, and his hands reached for his head covering his face.

"This is terrible… We'll make it our daily, after-dinner thing, what do you say?"

Her kiss answered his question.

"We could pull out some photos, those which didn't get stolen from me, and other things for a better illustration. Oh, I've always wished for this!"

He was thinking about writing a book dedicated to music, and their sessions would make it possible and easy. He told her and got another kiss.

She pulled an umbrella out of her pocket, and unfolded it. That gesture brought them even closer. The metaphor of protection against the rain, when they just decided to work on separate pieces but together, filled them with inspiration.

Every night there was so much to look forward to! Even the sad and tragic will be approachable, for both, she thought, and she could finally wrestle the monster without falling a victim to it.

For years, she pondered, she wasn't in any position to paint a big picture on a large canvas, and often plan even for a few months ahead, or weeks, and her moves thus appeared as reckless, sudden, and headless, irresponsible decisions. But her quick, urgent changes happened as a result of her awareness that she was being a target of the mad clock works, and for that very reason she couldn't look forward to anything. What a life!

"I know you are very forgiving," he sounded careful and gentle, almost singing. "Who hurt you most in your life? And would you be, or have you been able to forgive them?"

She was amazed by his capability to detect her emotions. She noticed how he steered their conversation skillfully and consciously on her theme, turning the limelight away from himself.

Sometimes she would joke, calling them Sherlock Holmes and Dr. Watson, often in attempt to restore a dialog.

"Dear Watson," she said with a sad smile, "I'd say... institutions, institutions created, and represented by people whether they worked on me directly, or remotely. I believe the people who became instruments of such institutions were damaged by the very institutions themselves. And we are at the beginning of our talk – my late father..."

"My dear Holmes..." was all he said. "Ideology, huh?"

"Yeah, 'seems like an ongoing war, a race of a sort into which is not advisable getting entangled. I still don't understand it, how it started, when, and who was involved, but I also resist the lure of it. 'Too much fascination by the evil'!"

"But we pay for it with our lives!"

"That's a fact. Think of that ink-pissing octopus apparatus."

"No way to see through."

He took over carrying the umbrella, and both glanced at the river surface, the color of which almost matched the color of the banks.

Vincent van Gogh used these colors for some of his water color paintings, brownish yellow and black and white. Her first published little book got one of these watercolor reproductions reprinted on the back cover. An open countryside, just like here. A satisfying, pleasant feel of a *déjà vu*. The birds took off without their noticing.

"Will it be too late for coffee?" he asked.

Neither of them wore a watch. She tried to locate the sun behind the clouds to guess the hour. In well known places she usually could tell the time with just a small inaccuracy.

"Maybe not."

"We'll have to warm ourselves up!"

"By all means!" she laughed.

It was a great gift they both were endowed with: easing out and plunging in, to and fro, serious matters, sandwiching them with the absurd stuff. They could take off the grown layers of protective shields in each other's presence, so much they trusted each other, and relied on that 'mirroring effect' of mutual receptivity, and instant harmony.

He sometimes retrieved himself into a shell. The hiding was caused most probably by the deep hurt and betrayal from the past. She never went there with him and often tried to make him come out fast, if she could not stop him from hiding there in the first place. From that solemn, internal retreat a new song was usually conceived, finding its way to the world like a newborn.

Ever since they shared space and life, his sadness was rather a rare event. His new music was usually conceived in the early morning after a good night sleep.

Each night's awakening yielded a safe and profound reflection. She understood well to what was happening, and enjoyed her quiet mornings overhearing the slivers of his play while she was making a breakfast, or dwelled inside herself.

With the muffled soundtrack she forgot about the surfaces and boundaries of own body infused into the music that was just being born.

In their minds, this was what they have fought for, this was happiness. Their close connection in both worlds, visible and invisible, like fluid in two connected containers cultivated their communion: the musical world, the vibrations audible only to the ears that know of solitude, introspection, and silent love.

They both were catching themselves at a delightful feeling of 'can't wait to get home', finding there little thoughtful things the other had prepared. For instance, if he came home first, he'd make sure her soft home shoes waited near the heater, so her feet wouldn't suffer cold. His methodical and reverend attention dawned on her after finding her shoes there every day.

At first she picked up on own odd feeling of questioning the absurd 'home slipper complex', and then quickly checked in the mirror if she appeared really, really old. But when she was hanging up carefully and with pleasure all of his sleek jackets, so they would sit nicely on his shapely, wide shoulders, she realized how *he* might feel about setting her soft shoes by the warm radiator.

She would preheat towels in the bathroom; it was one of his favorite rooms at home where he liked to hang out, 'preferably with you, dear', as he used to say. He'd often bring fresh, fragrant flowers without a reason. She'd use the old beer jug for a vase, and set up a table for a sit-down dinner, or any meal for that matter, even when he wouldn't wish to spend much time there. For her it was more symbolic, because there were many years she didn't own a table to eat at, let alone a bed.

He gradually began spending more time at the dining table, bringing with him work that was waiting on the floor while they ate; until she came up with a non-imposing solution not to make him feel obliged to please her, and got an old serving cart, without spoiling their enjoyable time, and without turning it into a routine.

She sensed he wasn't used to eating cooked meals, unless he made them himself. It was familiar to her too for different reasons; for years, she cooked only for herself.

Both of them consciously and silently noticed each other's past lacks which they called debts to one another, and tried to mend carefully by designed, thoughtful remedies.

"Best *objects d'art*, no?" he'd laugh while she was filling the old beer jug with water, and placing it ceremoniously as – grinning at herself for this colloquial expression – 'a center piece', soon moving it again to the side to be able to see across.

"I believe there are other *objects d'art* you like to look at, no?" she'd laugh back.

On the wall in his study, he'd often rotate different black and white photographs by Drtikol, certainly beautiful to look at.

While she was following this train of own thoughts, she was puzzled by the realization of how much they reflected memories of her father for years in oblivion, until her caring, most wonderful man and companion unearthed them by his artful questioning.

A long time ago, she was about eighteen, her father created a brief movement, not quite a dance called 'A Life of a Woman, a Life of a Flower'. She learned it by watching his smooth performance. Until now, this very minute, she never realized how far away he had gotten in his mind from this poetic image – a woman as a flower – in several decades.

What could possibly change him so much that in his last twenty years of life he appeared malfunctioning, as if operating on an automatic pilot which seemed to derail him from his original intentions? She knew about alcohol. She was suspecting him to having become an alcoholic for years. But there was something else. It was very frightening to know someone for so long, and witness such profound changes.

She sighed loudly, involuntarily, noticing that her companion was closely observing her profile.

"Yes, they are… you are my favorite."

"Oh! What are you talking about? It sounded like you just read my thoughts…"

"You are my favorite, Lily – of the River. My best heating unit," he laughed.

"Oh, Watson, are you instigating a radiator?" she emphasized in a British accent.

"Holmes, I am."

"Okay, coffee and a bath!"

Still quite a way from home, in the rain pounding on the umbrella, she now consciously stepped out of her thoughts, and yielded his presence fully, chastising herself for doing the work that could be done when alone.

Suddenly she felt overwhelmed by the silence shared with the man she had missed for most of her life, but who had been with her 'every step of the way' at all times; she quickly glanced at his partly covered face, hidden in the collar of the coat, and in the shadow of his black hat, revealing just his eyelashes flickering above the cheekbones. It was enough face for her to read.

She wondered what his quiet outside sounded like inside. She wouldn't disturb it by any insecure questioning, she just glanced peacefully again at his Watson's disguise.

"And beside institutions, *who's* hurt you? Meaning people," he insisted firmly.

She returned to the core of the mad clock machinery, and told him of her assumptions about the aspects of what she considered an all out war.

The analogies led to striking thoughts: the horrors of the Stalinist era, and its sophisticated, 'scientific' ways of tormenting people that the totalitarian regime used: punishing parents by not allowing their children to study, or succeed in any way, trying to corrupt them, and tug them to the opposite side, break their spirit by hard labor, those were Hitler's methods also. The possible origins of the hatred, and its fruit suggested that the enemy was the life itself, and the bearers of it – women, beauty, sovereignty, none of which can be owned, only loved. Madmen can't love; that implied a far reaching meaning.

"Think of a psychological war: a mother is caused enough pain if her very young daughter is taken away. She's slandered, scared by the paranoid regime, and its legal system in the midst of a divorce, rid of any opportunity to develop her significant talents, without a paying job, intentionally along the way; one can presume the emotional damage in that relationship, coldness, rejections, fear to approach by questioning one another that can never be healed, the truth never revealed? Let alone – if the child is taken away from her, and she never sees it again? Where to?

"What if her grown up daughter goes through similar motions in life, and the mother is in no position to turn it around, thus reminded all the time of her 'unsuccessful' fate passed on? How does that effect the mother-daughter relationships? Perhaps with a persistent cultivating of love, no matter what? In that sense I believe love is a non-negotiable gift, an illuminating blessing, because one needs almost inhuman strength and firmness of the spirit to come out in one piece. But how to express it from a distance, if not in words? And words aren't the best tool in such a case, are they? And what if, even if you find the words you'd like to say, the words can't be delivered?! Because you don't know where to send them? A Frenchman said 'There is no love, there are only symptoms of love.'"

He seemed so struck by her account that he stopped walking, and turned toward her outstretching his arms, almost in tears, feeling her pain. She fell into silence, regretting to have released so much, and so passionately at once. For a few minutes they just stared at each other, losing the sense of the place: the softly sloping river bank holding in heavily flowing yellowish waters.

She let out a long deep breath, unable to spell out even an apology for her question.

"Did you ever blame your father for anything in this matter?" he asked softly. She shook her head.

"Isn't it the worst thing in the world to be stolen love from?" and tears leaped out from her eyes.

"It would, if it was a possibility. Love can't be stolen. A person can be lured away, misled by appearances, confused by lies, scared, made jealous, involved in destructive relationships, all that before he or she learns differently. But love is *the* essence, present all the time, that's what makes you rich…"

He unbuttoned his coat and pulled a pressed, folded batiste handkerchief out of his breast pocket, and handed it to her.

"Yes, all true," she blew her nose. "Relationships however need a daily physical presence, the touch, the voice, the eyes, that soulful fabric, or we fall apart, we develop illnesses from deprivation, those are the real heartbreaks, no?"

He slowly nodded; he knew very well what she meant. He's lost many friends along whom he admired, loved, worked with, traveled, partied, argued, often because their relationship was no longer healthy.

He would care for a self-destructive person to see his or her decline, and endangered his own well-being, realizing he was in fact contributing to their weakness by his selfless compassion, instead of reaching out for his soulful needs. They became dependent on him emotionally, exploiting his huge heart. Sometimes it was a matter of life and death. To cut off someone like this cost him a load of guilt, before he learned to care about his own welfare, first quoting her letters frequently in his mind, her philosophical words about own burdens.

She knew him well also from the fragments of remembered statements made often in laughter, or in a dismissive manner, or from his willingly given interviews, always spoken in a tone as if he was talking with her. At least that's how it felt – one reason were the relevant references to her experiences described in her letters to him.

His interviews started to bother certain people without doubts who might have detected that personal tone of voice, and became involved in looking over her shoulder through the lenses along with the mad clock maker. How and when did it all start? It surely was maddening, as he said.

"You know what I cherish most between us? And it's something I remember you proclaimed when we were kids."

"What is it? Was I ever smart back then?"

"Were you smart?! You were in love, and that makes one sharp and wise, you know? Even at a very young age!"

"So what was it? I can't wait…"

"You said you really liked that you could tell me anything, everything."

"Trust."

She nodded.

"It's much easier to trust when we are young. So, if I say the same thing to you today, it's got a lot more weight. It's still based on the unquestionable trust. And I love being silent with you as well!"

He usually didn't want to owe anything, and in his generosity, he overpaid back:

"It's been always such a delight to be with you… so direct,

gentle, true..."

"There's no need to finding all the words, I feel the same... Once near, there's no fear, no struggle!"

She was handing him back his handkerchief, then blew her nose again, and stuffed it in own pocket.

"I'll wash it for you, Watson."

"My turn doing laundry, Holmes."

"I'll iron it."

"Unnecessary..."

"I like ironing your shirts, 'see, when they don't go to the cleaners, I always get to think about lovely things..."

She laughed and sneaked her gloveless hand into his pocket. He smiled and got hold of her hand inside the pocket firmly. She thought of his lyrics about holding hands being their home. He thought about holding their hands gloveless for the first time, a long time ago.

They hid under the umbrella and continued walking. Home, she thought to herself, home... their home.

"Do you remember that beautiful old film about the cat that wore magical spectacles, and everyone who was about to lie spoke the truth instead?"

She remembered it, and reminded him how the film ended up on the black list, locked up during the oppression, considered dangerous.

"It's basically a fairytale, no?" he wondered.

"You're right."

"Fairytales are dangerous?"

"For their revealing of the truth and happy endings. For bringing out joy and laughter as well."

"Amazing... The character of the male cat was an animation, or something advanced for the time in the combination with live actors, no?"

She agreed again.

"I often think you've got that gift of unveiling people's true nature like that cat with the magical spectacles. Am I right?"

"Maybe so, it used to cause me terrible problems. I am in essence a Hussite," she laughed. "Their motto was 'Speak the truth, love the truth, fight for the truth, believe in the truth...' And you know how Master Jan ended up."

"Like Joan of Arc," he mumbled. She paused, and then added a point:

"There were times, when I felt I was stuffed in a wash machine, in a centrifuge, pushed and pressed away from anything I was trying to do: going where I wanted and needed to be, finding a decent dwelling, work, earn money, start a business, teach, not to mention own field. It became impossible to find any, even low-paying work. 'Overqualified. Bad economy', I heard all the time... Any place I tried.

"Anything I put my heart into got spoiled, or was subjected to so much stress and pain, as if forcing me to abandon it all together, whether concerning people or activities. Not to mention love, 'see. I could even picture that my fondness and affection were somehow measured, and in whomever I took a liking, they got hurt, similar to the cattle that get a dose of electrical current to learn where is the fence... I've always been on the verge of becoming homeless, by the way."

"It happened to me many times, especially when I no longer wished to listen to what some people wanted me to do, think, feel, and say. I know how it goes."

"When I noticed a pattern, I understood: this also fell under the jurisdiction, so to speak, of the mad clock works. Obviously, someone decided to make me not only homeless, but also penniless, ill, heartbroken, and so desperate that all left for me would be the desire to die. Or exist like the Flying

Dutchman, destined to hopelessly sail the seas against the wind, never land. Sometimes his ship can be seen at the Cape of Good Hope, the legend says."

She paused, then tilted thoughtfully her head to his shoulder and added:

"Isn't that more or less the fate of all of us, immigrants? The whole world seems on foot, fleeing, these days, or rather years, or how about centuries!"

"Or someone was trying to make you do what *they* wanted, didn't they?"

"Hmmm. I have also observed over time a 'playful and clever' aspect of this madness, someone wanted to display their proud intelligence, a heartless lust for power over someone else, a sheer arrogance – in trying to play a god. A god with a chain of command, which along the way got corrupt. Something like the Fallen Angels, with the pleasure of being able to manipulate remotely, invisibly, utilizing technology. Ridiculing art, the creative process, inspiration, freedom, independence, suggesting that it was all but illusion, that someone was just pulling strings, and I was their puppet."

"How was that?"

"As a form of torture. Administering a vengeance. Using astrology, perhaps? Knowing people's birthdays, and using a clever software to 'predict' events in their lives with the frightening accuracy... Mind games to drive me crazy, or 'drive me to drink' as you said once. That way stealing from me would be justified, you see, if – in their view – I was just a puppet, and they manipulated everything I was doing: my writing, for example...

"Another 'tool' I've noticed: applying scientific theories like the Law of Attraction, or creating a 'parallel world'. Just like we experienced for so many years with the invisible Iron

Curtain and the symbolic, very visible Berlin Wall. Completely secluded, unperusable two worlds – for the two of us, lately based on fame and the lack of it, wealth and poverty, a respected social position and 'outside the society'... I came to the conclusion that even if we lived in the same town, not a city, a town, small town, the Hate Machine would prevent us from running into one another."

She paused as if she needed to gather more strength to say the most frightening observation:

"And sometimes it felt as if I 'became' you... I wrote about a similar idea in one of my stories, and I questioned whether you 'became' me at the same time by the law of the parallel worlds, designed by the Hate Machine, and what that might mean."

He looked shocked. Something has dawned on him, something he needed to think about, backtrack systematically, something which had been happening for long decades.

"You know well I don't care about these attributes in people!" he exclaimed.

She nodded, but his warmth wasn't the issue, their possible total impossibility to connect anywhere in the world was, on any platform: physically, or long distance, and through the internet in the most recent years.

She tried to explain that to him using many real examples of how the parallel world theory was applied in her view, based on her experiences, until she could see how upset with the evidence he'd become.

"Please, don't forget, this is going to be a story!" she reminded him. "The last thing I wish is you to be upset now!"

"But why would anyone want," he gasped.

"It's all about love and hatred, understand?"

"No. But I am glad you persist in telling me. Lots of time is lost, because I had no understanding, I had no idea ..."

She added hesitantly:

"Imagine a 'someone' with such a lust for power that *they* would invent a – let's say – a chess game where they could play with real people and 'live!', in an unlimited time frame, instead of the ivory figures, the black and white check board, and the commonly agreed rules upon... "

He slowed down all of his movement in a tremendous suspension.

"I see now WHY," he whispered.

"Yes, this is why so much time has passed, at least that's what I believe to be the facts."

They both ceased exchanging any more words, feeling united by the overwhelming meaning. Yes, it was becoming to make sense, the WHY...

Still... but *why*, why at all? Any single jealous person, or two, or a bunch of them could not have the power to create a mad clock works, the Hate Machine, controlling every move of not only an individual, or two, or more – but their whole area, even a city, or set events in motion this way. How? This was really maddening, incredible, monstrous, and virtually unimaginable!

"I can see how you can rely upon literature, making this into a story which people will regard as fiction," he remarked.

"The fabric of it being so very real..."

"I need to know for sure it has dissolved! No one deserves to lose two thirds of their lives due the mad clock works, Holmes!"

"Dear Watson, I wish I knew. The only thing I can confirm is that its malicious and destructive forces no longer trigger chain reactions, or mock what I do, feel, think, write, read and such. You know: 'Anything you say can (and will, ha, ha!) be used against you', kind of thing."

He looked at her gravely, weighing the words, and then

made a wavy gesture connecting them together as if saying – it must be so, otherwise we wouldn't be walking together in the rain. They came to a fork on the path and he pointed to a direction:

"Let's wait a bit; it's becoming cats and dogs."

"That's another thing – weather," she commented scanning the gray sky, "the mad clock works at times seemed to be somehow related to weather, or its satellite-based forecasts, think about it! The mad machine could manifest that way its manipulation to an observant person, and the machinists could laugh, how impossible it was to trace their mad clock works, and do something about it."

He followed the path, staying alert to her narrative. With the increased velocity of their steps, her breath filled her voice. She connected the Hate Machine created weather patterns with people's behavior: as if they were more often under the spell of words, and a gamble of their letter content, rather than under the unpredictable conditions of rapidly changing winds.

The wind began blowing stronger, and her memories of some of these irrational experiences came to the surface. Within the walking distance, suddenly a taller structure came into their view, set in a random group of old, leafless trees. His accelerated, brisk steps led her there. After a few guesses of what they were headed toward, she surprisingly realized it was a windmill. Or it used to be one. The big cross was no longer spun by the wind for some mechanical reason, she thought.

He explained to her that the original windmill was built by a real Dutchman with the intention to start over in a free country about three hundred years ago, but many inhabitants and owners lived there since. A more recent family feud left the building abandoned with the windmill arms firmly reattached, meant perhaps as a tourist attraction.

179

The building began to severely dilapidate. Unfortunately, the latest situation on the real estate market suggested the restoration cost might pose more liability than an asset, so the building's future remained uncertain. Even a sign forbidding trespassing was missing.

The trees around must have been growing for a long time, exceeding thrice the tall building, shaped like the Greek letter 'Pi'.

"But as a temporary shelter – if you're not too drenched and cold – it might be okay."

He touched her face with his, and both released a laughing cadence because their cheeks felt the same – *cold*! His warm hand covered almost her whole face. She shivered not from the difference in warmth, but from affection.

"And how about you, aren't you feeling cold?"

He shook his head and pushed his hat high with one finger which was her gesture using an imaginary hat to express 'what?!', and exclaimed:

"I hate outdoors!"

Of course, he didn't mean it, and thrust another one of his proverbial laughs. It rolled across the open space toward the river. Then he quietly read in her smiling face observations about his high sitting hat.

Inside the empty, a little spooky mill full of dusty shadows, a sturdy, well preserved staircase led to the top floor with more light where a view of the river opened through an unbroken window.

She supposed he knew the place well from before, but waited for him to share that with her if he wished so – or not. She shook off the soaked umbrella, and placed it on the old wooden stair landing.

He brushed off the wide window sill of the whitish dust

which she identified as ancient flour remnants – hm, a miller's house, and they sat down. For a while, they both just listened to the tapping rain, stared at the bubbles popping up in the puddles below, and watched the distant river flow.

He must have been thinking about this for some time, because when he spoke, his voice expressed a lot: a concern, pain, nostalgia, familiarity, and embraced even an anticipated answer, and the question was:

"Did you feel haunted?"

She was surprised by the sudden, from the sky fallen question, but even more by his repeatedly intelligent, acute sensibility, his gift of connecting with her.

"Someone perverted used your lyrics to haunt you, and my writings to haunt me, and laughed at us both," she said quietly, picturing the windmill cross. Analogically, an image from one of his music videos, featuring him kneeling at a cross, meshed in the reality.

She shared in short with him her experiences from the times she had finally got hold of his work which in most cases took a few years for various reasons, mainly financial. Also, her moving kept her busy, and without fresh news.

"Do you have an example?" he wanted to know.

"Yes. I wrote a sonnet, inspired by my desire of the wind bringing you… to me," she whispered and quickly glanced at him, because her book of sonnets was supposed to be a surprise for his birthday, and she just revealed its existence for the sake of the truth.

His eyes reflected such fondness when he returned his silent response by facing her, that she relaxed and continued.

"In a couple of days, a magazine printed photos of the local celebrities, or their girlfriends with 'windy' hairdos, meant as festive creations for attending a Christmas gala party. Of course you *not* being there, but rather very far away."

"You've always inspired new ideas, why not in fashion?" he tried to joke.

"I couldn't help by that point feeling watched, especially in anything related to you, 'see? I began deeply worry that whatever I was doing was being used not only against me, but against you as well," she replied.

There are all kinds of shapes of a cross, ran through her mind simultaneously, the Egyptian ankh resembling a human that also reminds of a key, or the Greek 'Tau', or Latin 'T'. For a very good reason she saw that 'T' in her head laying on the ninety degree angle, knocked down.

He was staring motionlessly out of the window, closely listening, while there in a muddy puddle a whole flock of tiny birds enjoyed their bath.

"Do you know it by heart?"

She raised her eyebrows and wrinkled her forehead, not immediately following, and then she nodded.

"Do you want to hear it?"

He nodded. She recited the sonnet that played with words, rhyming also his name's diminutive.

"Sounds archaic in our mother tongue, doesn't it," she stumbled back into English.

He shook his head. His eyes expressed a lot of emotions mixed together as always, when he was touched to the core, and wanted to give back what he got.

In the meantime, the rain tapered off, and turned into a fine mist. The birds' excited early spring chirping penetrated the closed window. He outstretched his arm, and released the latch. Air!

"Oh, how lovely!" she sighed. "What would be the world without birds?! What would be the world without music?"

"Look!" and he aimed his head to where the sun was about to break through the clouds.

The shiny world got embraced by golden-rosy vapors, the branches of the barren trees from which the water was dripping resembled festive garlands, decorated with chains of all the colors there are as the sun rays twinkled in every single droplet.

The crown to this spectacle arrived when a rainbow arch bridged the almost black sky on the opposite side to the sun. The river from the high view also changed colors, reflecting the heavy sky.

"This must be the old Dutchman's hello, waving with both arms," said she and crossed her arms waving for several times; with her legs standing wide apart, she marked an 'X'.

Almost intoxicated by the view, she praised the moment:

"What a painting, look at the light!"

His eyes glared happiness when he appreciated the light effects on her face, and noted:

"You haven't lost anything!"

He took her by surprise, but to catch up with his quick thinking, she borrowed a metaphor from the rainbow, the colorful, sudden, and 'out-of-nothing' phenomenon.

"You told me the same once before… on a hopeful date… do you remember? It held me together for many years."

"What is it that you miss about youth?" he asked her gently.

She needed time to answer; it wasn't coming lightly, because she needed a context. She wondered why he asked that question.

"I've always worked hard on not to be disconnected with myself at any age, and if you asked me at a different time, my answer would be probably each time different. I can say though one thing – I miss the luster of a *décolletage*, I'm sure you know exactly what I mean," she grinned.

"No, I don't," he answered sincerely.

She described the skin's soft reflection of the light resembling moonlight, or the glimmer of pearls, right under the neck, and above the breasts in a deep cut *décolletage*. The woman's chest allows the light to land on an angle, and softly glow.

"Now you know, right?"

He nodded and appreciated her lovely and fresh use of words:

"You have a way with words... that's what my dad used to say about your writing."

"Thank you, my dear Watson."

"You glow from the inside out," he finished. "You haven't lost anything."

"Thank you... And may I ask you what is it you miss about youth?"

He laughed, and tilted his head thoughtfully, weighing the question, scrolling to a truthful answer.

"My young bones," he shook his shoulders, as if that was all he found missing. "Exuberant energy, perhaps."

"Youth is so wasteful, isn't it?" she smiled including herself. She immediately considered unobtrusive remedies for his 'old bones'.

"I believe your bones have turned rather smart, not old."

"How's that?"

"Well, you move in the same graceful way I remember about four, five decades ago, still like dancing, but with more efficiency and sovereignty! And – be sure of one thing, I'd care for you even if you couldn't walk at all."

He lowered his head, something he always did when he felt deep love. Oh, here he goes again, moving me to tears! was what she felt.

A sudden shadow fell in from a dark cloud, threatening with another batch of cats and dogs. He closed carefully the window. She folded slowly the umbrella, and glanced around to hint if there remained any *dominus loci* after the old Dutchman. The room was empty, full of the white dust. The miller's house. She didn't like the feel.

"Do you think the Dutchman was a miller?"

"Perhaps."

There came another analogy: the saying about God's mills grinding slowly, but surely. In their mother tongue and culture people used the metaphor with a bit of emphasis on the regretful 'slowly', followed by an ominous pause before finishing with the definite 'but surely'.

"I felt so out of place at those times of my returns, listening to people's stories, complaining, gossiping, often hopelessly beyond repair with their vindictive attitudes. What's the word for being glad to hear about, to see, or to set up someone's disaster?"

As they stepped out into the fresh air again, she told him, adding that there was no equivalent in English.

"Right. Amazing," he shook his head.

She longed to have a little discourse on 'forgiveness' which in their native tongue originated in a different mode of thinking, more a passive letting go off. In a sense, it defined 'the national character' if there is such a thing, indeed. English on the other hand suggested, at least by her opinion, a lot more deliberating and feeling through, dealing with all sides of the pain, guilt, hurt, ill will, including the legal agenda, and offered something. 'For-give'.

He mentioned another word in their language for forgiving that expressed just as much. Admitting she had forgotten about that word, she told him how much she admired his beautifully refreshed mother tongue.

"Thank you… I agree with you. Sweeping stuff under the

rug, and too quickly, has been my big lesson in life," he concluded.

"That's because you are tolerant, unsuspecting malevolence," she reached for his face and caressed it.

"It's harder for you because you can see through people's intent, the cat with the magical spectacles deal; you 'connect the dots', something people don't commonly do here."

"Unless they are paid for it…"

He laughed and teased her:

"You've lost one thing – if you've ever had it: any sign of coming from a small country!"

"Did you want to say – provinciality?" she roared with laughter so much that all the bathing birds flew away.

He lowered his head forgetting about his hat, feeling caught at an imperfect expression. His hat flew away, and jumped into the puddle.

"Oh, no! I felt guilty for scaring the birds away by laughing, but your hat would have done it!"

"Well, your laughter was first – for the good reason I gave you," and he swiftly picked up his hat shaking off the water.

It reminded her of seeing Nezval, the poet, chasing his black bolder, blown off his head on a deserted sidewalk when she was about eight years old. His silhouette under his dark coat resembled a penguin; the strong wind made his hat hop, and the poet hopped too, trying to catch it.

The image opened up the whole theme about their common infatuation with poetry of the Twenties. While they were quoting authors, and their favorite poems of all the different languages, she back-flashed at the mad clock works' fragmentation efforts, corrupting language as well, her worries about what happens to the brain if not reading, not memorizing with such an easy access to the vast amount of information at hand with just 'a click of a mouse'. She compared the level of education their parents' generation with theirs.

He expressed hope, an eternal optimist, that people never discard books; the ritual of reading being so intimate, and enriching! He began to read, because he was missing her knowing how she liked books.

"Do you remember what you gave me for my fifteenth birthday?" she asked.

He looked surprised, and labored in his head; finally admitted he didn't. She hinted – as it often happened so – he might be wishing to hear her version, and enjoy listening to all of the facets of her voice and the choices of the words.

"It was a book."

He was so surprised he looked breathless.

"Oh, really? Do you remember which?"

She nodded and paused, anticipating his huge reaction.

"The Song of the Songs."

His eyes blinked in disbelief, and she thought – oh, he forgot how wonderful he's always been! Her smile finally reflected on his face. He was hoping that her whole recollection would take place.

She endowed him with an embrace, and told him about that long, grayish day they spent together, the flowers, and mainly about the charcoal illustrations accompanying the book. How honored and privileged she felt by his thoughtfulness, his delightful way to tell her how much he loved her.

When an extraordinary moment shines through the struggles in our life, the nature often plays along, and creates a backdrop: the sun broke through the dark clouds, the wind pushed them aside, and the world got illuminated by the sun's slanted rays. The day was coming to an end, and so was their walk, crowned by one of the most beautiful early memories they shared.

Through all this quite nostalgic, but rich and happy recollection a thorn of pain poked into her guts with one other strong, related, instant realization. She managed not to reveal it to keep the man walking aside of her immersed in his delightful discovery.

It's one thing to refresh own memory, and be reminded of ourselves by someone whom we know perhaps better than ourselves, but it's an entirely different thing to look back with today's eyes, having lived through so much, and realize we still love the way we used to, wiser than before!

That sudden, tarnishing recollection was about her father asking her later what was the birthday gift, how his eyebrows rose when she told him, how he wanted to see the book. Her father wouldn't take the book away from her, or censor it by a feeble parental sermon as usually; a father, who as a parent inconsistently, but strongly required respect for his authority, while at other times his attitude was quite liberal, at least that was how he seemed. He wasn't even forty then.

Her father witnessed this act of love and understood it. He experienced it as a blow. It was his jealousy, resembling God's jealousy described in the Old Testament, a kind of institutional jealousy, demanding an absolute obedience.

She tried, but couldn't remember any words he might have said. She was always quite precise in recording feelings, and own gut voice. Responsive she was, sensitive to emotional resonating. Later, she became aware of another, argumentative and tugging, foreign sounding internal voice which was trying to override this deep, and quiet voice resonating with the truth.

As happy and proud she was that day, her father's silent reaction froze it, till it resurfaced naked just now. She could see it all now, because of the talk during the soulful outing with her companion. That's where her father's jealousy began she believed, right there and then.

The man walking by her asked:

"There is something else, isn't it?"

She hesitated to vent her revelation, but his quiet voice spoke with so much urgency that she felt obliged to at least hint that 'something else', and not treat with avoidance his continuous interest, but appreciate his sensitivity to her emotions.

"Yes. It's about my father's dark side. His jealousy."

Her eyes blinked to absorb the excessive moisture.

"I am very grateful for our long walk today. It has unearthed lots of quite forgotten stuff. Thank you, my dearest Watson."

"You're welcome, Holmes, as always! Don't forget: you can tell me anything, everything!"

He pulled his keys out of the pocket, pushed his black hat back a little, and asked her:

"Do you like marbles?"

She rapidly blinked her eyes several times, this time from being quite puzzled:

"What?… What marbles?"

He released a roar of silent laughter from the marvelous mix of reasons: her sweet confusion, the hilarious moment born from 'the charm of the unwanted', the double language joke, and of course, the looking forward to his coffee and bath.

"When the puddles dry up, we can go play," he answered innocently.

It got established as a non-written rule when they took a bath together to enjoy it in silence, and often with their eyes closed, or in very dim lights.

One reason for that were the sensations they experienced from the touch, and by ear. And the reason for that was that they felt so indebted to one another over so many missed years of not being together, but wishing otherwise that such bathing almost gained a status of a regular party of a special sort.

As when they were children holding each other's hand, now as well, their hands helped them to express a lot more than words. Their hands have been always their asset in the quiet communication, whenever they could see each other during those years of deprivation.

This silent language resembled the expressiveness of the hands from the Oriental parts of the world where women wear black robes covered from head to toe, hiding sometimes even their eyes, only their bare hands show. The gestures accompanying the speech have evolved with a high refinement, saying what the face can't.

Disturbing, no doubt, but she also thought of the Thousand and One Night Tales she loved to read as a child, full of rare scents and fragrances, dangers overcome by the swift spirit, helpful ocean and air creatures, long journeys in hot sand, the fata morgana of the refreshing oasis, colorful markets, tall minarets, shadowy viziers, and smart women.

Their hands have aged, veins pronounced, the tops of the hands weathered like old wood. Spots and scars, sometimes roughness of the skin from cold, dry season conditions enhanced, and exaggerated the age.

But – as the saying about the glass half full or empty goes – their soft, supple palms grew even more gentle and caring in touch, as if they could see with them, expressing subtlety. The gestures have augmented in richness, influenced by their creative professions, and fueled by ever present, deep emotions.

She has always affectionately watched his hands' and arms' movements. His hands were large, well suited for a musician. The flow of his energy expressed through his body language spoke of his feelings which he was always in touch with. Such a rare and exquisite state of heart for a man! She admired his courage for staying in such a state, not escaping from feeling so much pain, and not being numbed by it either. The realm of music was his refuge and oasis.

In the lowered lights, they listened to the little sounds, and watched their muffled preparations for the bath, attending each other. A sudden *'déjà vu'* resurfaced in her mind.

One beautiful late spring day – his parents were absent, working abroad at that time – they spent all day together swimming in a pond, took a walk in the fields, then listened to the singles on his parents' record player, snuggled together on a couch. When the night fell, he turned off the record player on the other side of the room, disrobed there completely, and tiptoed back to her. Then he gently helped her out of the tight dress. They held each other in the arms for hours.

She never forgot those light, quick rustling sounds, and her feelings about what she had pictured with her eyes closed, listening to him. It was before she got the Song of the Songs, she thought. She missed the last bus home that night, the phone stopped working. He called her house to explain the situation to her father who demanded them both to come immediately. There was no other option than to spend the night in his house.

The next morning they both rode quietly together on the bus and streetcar to her house, her father was already gone for the day. She remembered thinking how it would be wonderful, if the two of them could live under one roof, and no one would interfere. Her father was furious, and wouldn't talk to her for days.

In a few days, she was leaving town for vacations, he came to say good bye and kissed her in front of both of her parents who happened to accompany her. She remembered their astonishment. He visited later her father bravely at home to apologize, and wrote her a beautiful letter about it. As most of his letters, this one as well, got stolen from her – through out the years – by other jealous people.

She thought – if that parallel world theory, applied by the mad clock works, was running in both of the worlds simultaneously, then her letters got stolen from him too... but she didn't want to ask him now about it.

At this moment, their quiet enjoyment of the bath together was appropriate for the precious, communicative silence. Her inquiring if he remembered that day, her curiosity about the existence of her letters would be more suitable for one of their evening sessions.

She fully concentrated on their relaxing, restful bath, and his hands, playing her as well as any of his musical instruments.

"Tell me about your mother's fury," he said, sipping coffee, and his entertained expression made her question the reason for his seemingly disjoined, underlined, and a little private laugh. Then she noticed he was sitting down on the rug barefoot.

Before she opened her mouth to respond, she pulled off her socks, and stretched her bare feet toward his. Their feet were similarly shaped as if they were truly related. He made the same observation. It erased his private, inner laugh: how come he hadn't seen it before?

She suddenly heard one of his oldest songs in her head, thinking he possibly couldn't have known Shakespeare that well yet, let alone in English, and the film version of that particular comedy wasn't made yet with one of his favorite actors, Richard Burton. Katharina wasn't prepared to dance at her sister's wedding barefoot. A colloquial expression.

Her voice came out like a sound of a trumpet with a plunger, submerged, when she answered:

"Mom was trying to conquer her fury creatively, and learn how to …'love an enemy'."

She wasn't very satisfied with her laconic words.

"What I've seen evolving on her spiritual path during the last years," she expanded, "was that her self-training of fifty years has specialized. She's been studying the Sephardic nation."

"Does she have anything against the Jews?" mumbled he his question in surprise at that conclusion.

The statement she made sounded illogical, as far as he knew her mother: a lady well read in quite a few languages, musical, at her age acute in judgment, up-to-date, coherent, and very brave, while he was picturing her playing Chopin in the room alone.

He didn't know the room was a former kitchen, converted into her sister's room with an extra bed for her visiting every fortnight, the kitchen moved, wedged in the hallway as a 'kitchenette'. He never accompanied her inside her mom's home.

Only many times he rode all the way with her on the old, clinking streetcar like a true gentleman. Then all the way back by himself – it took at least two hours back to his house late night which he'd spent by reflecting on their sparkly date, and falling more in love.

"No, of course not. I believe, she would have a particular bad one in mind. Hatred isn't in her nature. Anger and fury, yes, when she sees beloved people subjected to injustice, and years of persecution, once she realizes it.

"I know, a persecutor being a member of a traditionally persecuted nation, what can one say! When she says stupidity is probably the worst of human faults, she refers to her own realization – which I'd call a life in fog; it's not respectful to blame oneself for unknowable things. So, since early on, she'd found her way how to relate to some very painful matters through music."

"This method could be applied as a remedy to the ills of the world. Your mom is wise."

He paused and then uttered:

"I have my own parallel."

"I know you do, my dear."

"She understands you well, doesn't she," he rerouted the conversation back to her mother, finishing his coffee.

"I think she does. Lots of hard, silent work. Just suffering through many years counts, you see. Lots of reflectivity, solitude, tears, and quiet loving. Because of our fate, her unnecessary guilt. How could a private, young individual win against a totalitarian institution? In short, it caused us much pain from unspoken reasons which I haven't dared to inquire about due my respect for her age, and her well deserved peace."

After a brief, deliberate silence, he gently asked with tenderness in his voice:

"Can you play Chopin?"

She shook her head.

"No. No excuse, except that for years, with occasional breaks, I had no musical instrument available, so, no practice."

He looked at her sideways with an almost unnoticeable grin:

"Now you do."

She took a big breath in and released it with enchantment:

"You'd let me?"

He nodded.

"And... will you teach me if I practice?"

He nodded again, while she blushed realizing what she just asked from this master composer. But what he had in mind was his invention of own Magical Clock Works, and he wasn't yet ready to reveal it to her.

"No need for fury, nor Chopin, my dear!"

He began – as he did on rare occasions – telling her about music, in his plain way, using simple words, but she knew very well those words represented a tip of an iceberg, a huge amount of work, experience, listening, composing, and finding ways to express, which meant also lots of yielding.

She wouldn't interrupt his erudite, yet not patronizing lesson for anything! Her admiration for music composition as for any art creation was coming from understanding its complexity by analogy: if one yields enough by being true to one's heart, one becomes a fine instrument, perhaps a God's messenger. She didn't believe he'd ever say such a thing about his music.

Overwhelmed and humbled, she listened; tears entered in her eyes from her throat, and calmly ran down her face. She only felt their warmth after the fact, and remained still, leaning somewhat uncomfortably supported by one arm not to distract him.

Perhaps he was sorting out his ideas for the book he was gathering courage and inspiration to write. Courage, because he was questioning whether he had much to say. But – just like with his very first solo album – once he started working on it, and recording the pieces thinking about its message, its cover, it all came beautifully together, and his insecurities about the outcome dispersed.

As he was speaking to her, moved by her tears solemnly falling on her hands, his idea of his Magical Clock Works began to unfold. He could never build it by himself. He needed her, no one else but her. There has been always a connection which kept them both alive for all those years, and perhaps this was the very reason.

He got so excited by this unique and powerful idea that he almost told her about it, but wisely he held off, and kept on initiating her into being his musical ally.

He didn't have to work very hard: her loyalty, interest, musical education, excitement, capacity for delight, all, were an asset. And she was, they both were excellent listeners.

"My first suggestion to you, my dear Holmes," he blinked at her, "would be – just listen. Listen to everything as if it is already music."

"Watson, I already am," she grinned.

"And then, you just feel it, or think it over as music yourself." She was gleaming, waiting for more, but that was it. Such a simple request. He let her ponder on it alone. She put into practice his suggestions immediately.

It worked easier with her eyes closed. The sounds were layered; some of them contained a pattern, or even a rhythm. She could hear her own heart. In the distance, one last bird was calling it quits.

When he came back, she was fast asleep. He sat down by her and watched her breath raising her chest, her calm, absent face, her relaxed arms and hands, her crossed legs, and touched her bare feet lightly. She would hurt her back, if she stayed on the floor all night, her feet were getting cold.

Her cat nap gave him a reason for composing a lullaby. Before she woke up, he was finished with his lyrics, and the beginning of the song, and the refrain.

"Watson! I was thinking music!" she stretched.

"I did see it… far fetched, huh, Holmes?!"

"Hm. And what have you been doing?"

"I've done the same."

"Have you seen me there?"

He nodded, smiling:

"I sure have, in fact I'd followed you there…"

He opened up his yellow notebook and jotted down quickly a few words. Then he pulled her up by hands, and concluded:

"…and now, you'll follow me!"